Molly had the sense that someone was watching her.

And not in a good way. These eyes from the dark weren't the gaze of an admirer. She glanced over her shoulder and saw no one. Hustling across the dark car park, the high heels of her boots hit the asphalt with hard clicks. Was she imagining danger? Or did she have real cause for alarm? It was smart to assume the latter.

Parked a couple of spaces from her car was a white van—the type of anonymous vehicle used for deliveries. She didn't see a logo on the side. Suddenly, a tall figure dressed all in black leapt out. The face was a blank—hidden behind a ski mask. In the gloved hand of the attacker, Molly saw the gleam of a blade.

Self-defence lessons from Adam told her to aim for the knees, groin or throat. And to make noise. With a loud yell, Molly kicked. With another yell, she yanked open the door to her car. If she could get inside, she'd be safe. As quickly as he appeared, her attacker va

Someone was

Rocky Mountain Manoeuvres

CASSIE MILES

SILHOUETTE®
INTRIGUE™

To my marriageable daughters, Signe and
Kersten. And, as always, to Rick.

*Silhouette and Colophon are registered trademarks of
Harlequin Books S.A., used under licence.*

*First published in Great Britain 2006
Silhouette Books, Eton House, 18-24 Paradise Road,
Richmond, Surrey TW9 1SR*

© Kay Bergstrom 2005

*Standard ISBN 0 373 22832 5
Promotional ISBN 0 373 60485 8*

46-0806

*Printed and bound in Spain
by Litografía Rosés S.A., Barcelona*

CASSIE MILES

has learned a lot about the bridal biz from her children. Marriage planning is a fascinating and complex world where anything goes. Releasing live doves. Building centrepieces of fruit. Wedding cakes that are taller than the groom. Because so much can go wrong, a wedding is the perfect setting for suspense.

When Cassie reviews all the exciting wedding ideas she got while researching *Rocky Mountain Manoeuvres*, she comes up with one consistent conclusion for her children: "I'll pay you to elope..."

CAST OF CHARACTERS

Molly Griffith—A leggy blonde with a shady past, Molly has worked for Colorado Crime Consultants since its start seven years ago.

Adam Briggs—A former marine, Adam founded CCC. His dedication to fighting crime has left little time for a personal life.

Pierce Williams—He got into the wedding planner business using contacts he made when he was a Denver Broncos football player.

Gloria Vanderly—Pierce's ex-wife operates a bridal boutique that handles the most fashionable, extravagant weddings.

Stan Lansky—Gloria's tailor works hard on bridal gown alterations and original designs.

Denny Devlin—Once the premier caterer in town, his business has been struggling after an unfortunate setback.

Ronald Atchison—The flamboyant wedding photographer has many artistic interests on the side.

Lucien Smythe—His jewellery store provides loaned diamonds for many special events, including weddings.

Phil Prath—His name is on the lease for renting Pierce's classy loft in downtown Denver.

Chapter One

Midnight was the hour for lovers, dreamers and thieves. He waited patiently. Soon, it would be his time.

For an hour and thirty-three minutes, the thief had crouched in the shadows of landscaped shrubbery and dry autumn flowers. He had watched the well-lit rear entrance to a sprawling Tudor mansion owned by one of Denver's most prominent families. He had listened to bits of conversation as the French doors opened and closed.

Rubbing his gloved hands together, he shivered in the night chill. These people should be going to bed soon. They had a wedding tomorrow. They needed their rest.

The French doors opened again. The bride-to-be and her groom stepped outside. Unmindful of the cold, they strolled across the lawn and entered a gazebo that was only fifteen feet from where the thief was hidden.

He held his breath. Clad in black, he was invisible in the night. In any case, these betrothed lovers wouldn't notice him; they had eyes only for each other. The groom was tall and rugged. She was slender, blond and graceful. They whispered words of love. A soft murmur. A tender sigh.

Their palpable joy offended the thief. He loathed

these perfect people and their perfect lives. They had wealth, beauty and happiness. He had to struggle for scraps—working long hard hours and never getting ahead. Bitterness oozed through his veins like poison. His stomach cramped and he pinched his lips together, holding back his groans of misery and rage.

The bride-to-be gazed up at her betrothed and said, "It's late. You should go now."

Yesss. The thief mentally echoed her words. *Go now.*

But the tall, rugged man replied, "I don't want to leave you."

"After tomorrow," she said, "we'll be together."

"Forever."

Go now. Go now. The thief silently chanted.

A new plan occurred to him. He might not have to risk a break-in. When the groom-to-be departed and the front door was opened, the electronic burglar alarm system would be deactivated. The thief could slide in and out without a trace. It was as if they were inviting him to steal their most precious treasures.

He followed the lovers as they returned to the house. He paused on the flagstone terrace and peered through the windows on the French doors, watching as the young couple went toward the front of the house.

The thief's gloved hand rested on the door handle. An electric thrill surged through him. Would he be caught? Would he be safe?

Opening the door, he darted inside. From the front of the house, he heard people saying their goodbyes. In moments, the doors would lock and the alarm system would be turned back on. Quick action was necessary.

Silently, he entered a vast, opulent room. On long tables, the wedding gifts were displayed. Such an array! Such glittering riches!

He helped himself to a shiny stainless steel gravy boat, a matching butter dish and a toaster, placing the objects into the padded pillowcase he carried with him.

Quiet as a shadow, he crept across the plush carpet and returned to the night with his treasures.

FOR ONCE, the unpredictable October weather in Colorado had cooperated. The temperature hovered near sixty-five degrees, and the skies were a perfect cloudless blue. It was a gorgeous afternoon for an outdoor ceremony. A wedding!

Molly Griffith was delighted to be one of the guests. She loved weddings. She'd always been a party girl. From the time she was a kid, she enjoyed playing dressup in the highest of high heels and feather boas and all the sparkle she could get her hands on. That was still her favorite style.

For this event—a high society affair—she considered toning down. But why? *If you've got it, flaunt it.* And Molly had it. She might be past her twenties, but she could still turn heads. Today, her snug-fitting dress was colored in swirls that ranged from pastel to navy blue. The low, square neckline showed significant cleavage—one of her best features. Her bolero jacket had splashes of starburst sequins. And her long blond hair was upswept in curls that would have done Dolly Parton proud.

She liked standing out in the small crowd that had gathered outside the French doors at the rear of the Carradine mansion. These other guests were the so-called beautiful people of Denver. The jet-setters. The rich and famous. Their glittering pendants, earrings and bracelets were genuine diamonds, rubies and pearls. Molly's gaze fixed on a short woman, dressed in gray silk, with three carats on each earlobe. Wow! A regular person could buy a decent used car with those earrings.

The wedding decorations were bold and striking—scarlet and gold flowers with flashes of iris blue. On the lawn, a few rows of chairs faced a bower of red roses entwined with golden aspen leaves. That was where the ceremony would take place. From the terrace, a harpist played a rippling crescendo.

Weddings were just so beautiful! Molly beamed. "Isn't this sweet?"

Her companion, Adam Briggs, glanced at his wrist-watch. "Aren't they supposed to get started?"

"In twenty minutes," Molly said.

"How long do we have to stay?"

"We're invited to the reception."

"Swell," he muttered. "Fancy little sandwiches and fish eggs."

"Stop whining, Adam. You sound like a three-year-old kid."

However, as she glanced at him, she had to admit that he looked good. His three-piece charcoal suit was meticulously tailored. His trouser cuffs fell neatly over his polished black wingtips. His striped silk tie was in a perfect Windsor knot.

Adam's rigorous grooming was the result of the training he received in the Marine Corps, where he learned to hang all his shirts facing the same way, to visit the barber every three weeks and to align the buttons on his vest with the center button on his trouser waistband. He'd confided to her that one of the reasons he enlisted in the Corps was because they had the best uniforms. She responded with a suggestion that the Marines change their recruiting slogan to: The Few. The Proud. The Really Well-Dressed.

Adam hadn't laughed. He seldom did.

You can take the man out of the Marines, but you can't take the Marines out of the man. He'd retired from the military long ago and was now the head of Colorado Crime Consultants. For the past seven years, Molly had been his administrative assistant. Ironically, her early training and background were the direct opposite of Marine Corps discipline.

"You clean up well," she said. "You're very handsome today."

"Right." He stood at ease with his hands loosely clasped behind his back.

"Now you're supposed to say, 'Molly, you look nice, too.'"

"Nice." He nodded briskly. "I like blue."

She'd spent hours shopping for this outfit. In her humble opinion, she looked spectacular. And all Adam could say was, "I like blue."

She should have been accustomed to the lack of compliments. After their years together, he probably didn't even notice that she was female. If she sat behind her desk, completely naked and painted green, he wouldn't look twice.

Recognizing a friendly face in the crowd, she waved.

"Who's that?" Adam asked.

"You've met him before. Pierce Williams. He's the wedding planner."

"Interesting," Adam said.

Pierce was well over six feet, a little taller than Adam, and built like a brick wall, solid from the ground up. "He used to play for the Broncos."

"A football player," Adam said. "How did he end up planning weddings?"

"When he was a Bronco, he made outstanding social

contacts with people who had the bucks to hire planners. And Pierce always had a talent for throwing great parties."

"Beer bashes," Adam said.

"To start with," she conceded. "Then he graduated to these fancy affairs. It's all a matter of planning, you know."

She'd met Pierce years ago when they were both taking night school classes on organizational management. After class, they discovered that they had more in common than an appreciation for wedding ceremonies. Both were raised in the foster care system. Both had, in their youth, run afoul of the law. Both had turned their lives around.

She was proud of his success. Big, burly Pierce Williams had become Denver's premier wedding planner.

"Molly!" Pierce strode toward her. "Wow, babe. You look incredible."

She gave him a friendly hug. "I really like the decorations. They're totally autumn."

"How about the harpist?"

"Very classy."

"This is my favorite kind of event. Small but elegant." He grinned. "With an unlimited budget."

"Not to mention that the bride and groom are terrific people."

"How do you know Kate and Liam?" Pierce asked.

Adam replied, "Liam does volunteer work for CCC."

"Colorado Crime Consultants," Pierce said. A frown pulled at the corner of his mouth, and he lowered his voice. "I'm glad I ran into you two. I've got a problem you might be able to help me with."

"Tell me," Molly said.

"Theft." Pierce guided them to one side of the terrace where they could talk in relative privacy. "Last night, somebody broke into the house and stole some of the wedding gifts."

"Did you file a police report?" Adam asked.

"Not yet. I didn't want to disrupt the wedding day with a police investigation, and the stuff that was taken wasn't particularly valuable." His big hands gestured helplessly. "A gravy boat, a butter dish and a toaster."

Molly was intrigued. "Why would anybody steal stuff like that?"

"Beats me," Pierce said. "And this isn't the first time gifts have been stolen. At another wedding I planned, a robbery took place in the bride's home while everybody was out at the ceremony. Just last week, the thief struck at the reception after the wedding."

"What happened?" Molly asked.

"He stole a lady's wristwatch and a fancy pin. Cheap costume jewelry. Apparently, it happened during the dancing. There was an oldies band."

Knowingly, Molly nodded. A dance floor with everybody bouncing around and bumping into each other was tailor-made for picking pockets—a skill she'd used herself. "Was the watch valuable?"

Pierce shook his head. "None of the stuff that's been stolen is worth much. This thief is like a magpie bird, stealing shiny objects for his nest."

A magpie. Molly liked that comparison. She knew from experience that thieves came in many types, ranging from pathetically driven kleptomaniacs to slick professional businessmen who made a decent living fencing other people's belongings.

In her own situation, when she'd tried her hand at theft, she'd been dead broke and homeless. Desperate need had driven her to become a pickpocket. However, as she developed her skill, she discovered that she got a charge out of stealing. The whiff of danger made her life a little more exciting.

It was lucky for her that Adam had come along when he did. He'd caught her when she tried to lift his wallet. Instead of turning her over to the police, he gave her a respectable job. His influence put her on the straight and narrow, and she liked walking that path. She had vowed never to sink into crime again.

Sometimes, though, she missed the thrill.

"Pierce, this doesn't sound like a huge problem. A couple of trinkets go missing. So what?"

"It's bad for my business." He shrugged his heavy shoulders, shaking off the potential embarrassment of petty theft. "Anyhow, I thought maybe you and Adam could catch my magpie."

"Sorry," Adam said quickly. "CCC doesn't take on private investigations."

"Why not? I know this isn't a big deal, but it's still crime."

"You need the cops," Adam said. "Or you should hire a private eye. Not us."

CCC was a non-profit network of private citizens with special skills. Their occupations were varied: medical examiners, journalists, entomologists, photographers and psychologists. These people volunteered their talents to help solve unusual aspects of crimes—past and present. All investigations were conducted hand in glove with law enforcement agencies.

As the administrator of CCC business, Molly understood that focus and she knew that Pierce's problem didn't fall into their typical purview. But he was her friend. And she wanted to help him.

"Maybe," she said, "I could look into this for you. On my own time."

"Thanks, Molly." He leaned forward to kiss her cheek. "You're a doll."

"I'll come by your office on Monday morning."

He glanced at his wristwatch. "You two better take a seat. The bride is ready to get started."

As Adam escorted her to the chairs facing the rose bower, his posture was even more rigid than usual. Under his breath, he said, "I don't want you involved with Pierce's problem. CCC does not investigate petty theft."

"Maybe we should. We haven't been all that busy lately. Our last big case was the murder investigation with our charming bride and groom—Kate and Liam."

"A good example," Adam said. "Kate and Liam also chose to ignore my advice. They ran off on their own and nearly got killed. Just look what happened to them."

As the harpist played the opening notes to "The Wedding March," the guests rose and turned toward the house. Kate Carradine stood framed in the French doors. This was her second wedding, and she wore a long sheath in champagne gold satin. Her bouquet was red roses—vibrant colors that were eclipsed by the radiance of Kate's smile.

"Look what happened," Molly said, repeating Adam's words. "Seems like a happy ending to me."

"There's no way CCC can start taking on this sort of case. I forbid it."

She turned and glared at him. She couldn't believe he'd used the *F* word with her. Forbid? "What did you say?"

"You heard me."

Any doubts she might have had about investigating

the magpie for Pierce vanished. Though Adam Briggs was her boss, that didn't give him the right to forbid her from helping out a friend.

"Here's the deal," she said. "I'm going to help Pierce on my own time. I never take sick time, and Lord knows I've earned about a thousand days off. I'll work undercover to preserve the precious reputation of CCC."

"How?" Adam asked. "Pierce knows you. His friends know you. They're aware of where you work."

"All I need is a cover story," Molly said.

As Kate passed gracefully between the rows of chairs, she winked at Molly. For an instant, they shared the joy of true love fulfilled—an impossible dream that sometimes comes true.

Sunshine spilled gently into the yard. A gentle warmth touched Molly's face and penetrated deep inside her, heating the blood flow around her heart. True love. It was a wonderful thing.

Silently, she dismissed her thoughts about what a pain in the butt Adam could be. Life was too short to dwell on the negative. Might as well enjoy the moment.

Taking her seat, she knew exactly how she'd handle the investigation into petty theft for Pierce, the wedding planner. To Adam, she said, "I'll pretend that I'm spending time with Pierce to plan my own wedding."

"What?"

"You heard me, Adam. I'll be an undercover bride."

Chapter Two

On Monday morning, Adam pulled his 1995 white Land Cruiser into his assigned parking space behind the CCC offices. The time was 08:13.

He noticed that Molly's lavender Volkswagen bug was parked askew with the right rear tire overlapping the white line defining her space. Apparently, she'd been in a hurry or careless. Adam didn't care which. At least she was here.

He didn't know what to expect from Molly this morning. They hadn't spoken after the wedding on Saturday, which meant she'd had the rest of the weekend to stew. It was his hope that she'd reconsidered her harebrained scheme to investigate petty theft for her wedding planner friend. An undercover bride? What the hell was that all about?

Though Adam respected her intelligence, Molly didn't have sufficient training for field investigations. He'd tried to instruct her in hand-to-hand combat and the use of firearms, but she never took those lessons seriously. If she ran into danger, she'd be outmatched.

Nor did she have the patience required for interrogation. Molly was blunt and straightforward. There wasn't a subtle bone in her body. Which, in and of itself, wasn't a bad trait because it meant she was clear-thinking, able to see what was needed and to carry through. She was proficient at her administrative work. Here. Where she belonged. In the CCC office. At her desk.

He strode on the sidewalk circling the yellow Victorian house that had been converted into office space. In the flower borders at the edge of the verandah, only a few mums and hardy geraniums held their color in October. The lawn had faded to a dull winter green, but the grounds were tidy, swept clean of fallen leaves.

The location of this office in Golden—west of Denver—pleased him. Though Golden was home to the massive Coors brewery and Colorado School of Mines, there was a friendly, small-town feel to this area. The waitress at the Mesa Café knew he liked his burgers rare and his coffee hot. The dry cleaner used the right amount of starch on his shirts. Yet, the CCC office was less than half an hour's drive from metropolitan Denver, where there were all the conveniences of a big city. And all the crime.

Inside the foyer, he went through the first door on the right, entering the CCC offices. Molly sat waiting behind her oak desk, which was, as usual, well-organized and cleared of extraneous papers. Her bright red fingernails tapped an impatient rhythm on the desktop. She reached up to flip her long blond hair off her forehead. The expression in her blue eyes looked like trouble.

"Good morning," Adam said, ignoring her glare.

He marched directly to the coffee machine where Molly had already brewed his special blend of arabica and Sumatra beans. The dark liquid poured neatly into Adam's white mug with the Marine Corps emblem on the side. *Semper Fi.* At his desk, Adam knew *The Denver Post* would be waiting. He hoped to escape into his inner office without a conversation.

But Molly left her desk and blocked his way. Coolly, she said, "There are a couple of letters for you to sign. I left them on your desk. And I'll check in tonight to make sure everything is going all right."

"You're leaving?"

"I promised Pierce I'd help him out, and that's what I'm going to do."

Life was so much easier in the military. "What if I gave you a direct order to stay right here?"

"I'd tell you to write it in triplicate, fold it twice and shove it where the sun don't shine."

"You know, there's a thin line between sass and insubordination."

"So court-martial me." She grabbed the leopard-patterned purse that matched the furry collar on her jean jacket. "You have my cell phone number if you run into any emergencies."

Damn it! He didn't want her to go. "As a matter of fact, I have a special project for today. I need your help."

She paused at the door. "You need me?"

"Yes, I do."

Suspiciously, she said, "Tell me about this special project."

"My sister and her husband are going out of town for a few days, and I said I'd watch my two-year-old niece."

"Amelia." Molly smiled fondly. "She's such a little cutie-pie. It's hard to believe she came from the same gene pool as you."

"Nonetheless," he said. "You can see why I require your presence here today."

"As a baby-sitter?"

"I prefer to think of it as caretaking, wherein we provide suitable activities for—"

"This is a perfect illustration of our basic problem,

Adam. You don't take me seriously. I'm smart. I'm efficient. And I'm capable of a lot more than babysitting Amelia." Her blue eyes narrowed to laser-edged slits. "Or baby-sitting you, for that matter."

"Me?"

"That's right," she said. "You and your special blend of coffee. Your regular barber appointments every three weeks. Your oil changes on exactly the recommended mileage."

"Simple maintenance," he said.

"Nothing about you is simple. You require more caretaking than any two-year-old."

She pivoted in her high-heeled boots and slammed the door on her way out.

Just like a woman. She had to have the last word.

In this case, however, she was mistaken. He didn't take her for granted. Her work was high caliber, and he appreciated her efforts. Why the hell couldn't she see that?

Because he didn't tell her.

Adam scowled at the empty swivel chair where she should have been sitting. Her tidy desktop mocked him. The potted plants on the windowsill and the fern atop the file cabinets nodded in mute agreement with Molly. Apparently, he didn't tell her often enough that he appreciated her.

But why should he? He paid her salary and her health insurance. He cosigned when she bought her house. Damn it. What did she want from him?

As he turned toward his desk, the coffee slopped over the edge of his mug and spilled onto his shirt cuff. This was going to be a long, frustrating day.

MOLLY HAD NEVER been to Pierce's Cherry Creek North office before, and she was impressed by the tonal artwork and attractive, modern furniture that made a basic beige color scheme seem original. "This isn't what I expected," she said. "It doesn't look very wedding-ish."

"Did you think I'd have pink plaster cupids hanging from the ceiling?"

"Maybe cupids wearing Bronco jerseys," she said.

Though her husky friend was dressed respectably in a long-sleeved shirt and khaki trousers, he looked like he was still wearing his football shoulder pads.

"Follow me," he said.

He led her behind a partition to a well-lit space with a long conference table. Arrayed on a wall of shelves were sample books for invitations, caterers, cakes, color schemes and magazines filled with the latest trends. The opposite wall was covered with photographs of wedding decorations, table settings and bridal parties. Everywhere Molly looked was wedding, wedding, wedding. It was like a matrimonial explosion.

"This is more like it," she said. "By the way, I'm not doing this investigation under the auspices of CCC. I'm working undercover."

"How so?"

"While I'm collecting evidence, I'll pretend to be planning my own wedding."

"To Adam?" he asked.

Utterly aghast, she gaped at him. "Why on earth would you think that?"

"Well, Molly. It's kind of obvious that you two are—"

"Stop right there." Adam Briggs was the last man she'd ever consider as a potential groom. He was cranky, obstinate and constantly underestimated her. Just the thought of him made her so angry that she could spit. "If I'm going to have a fantasy fiancé, he's going to be a *real* fantasy."

"Tell me."

"His name is Rafael DuBois. Of course, he's a total babe. And he's a multimillionaire from Australia, which is why he won't be around while I'm planning our wedding."

Pierce held up his left hand and wiggled his fingers. "What about your engagement ring?"

She frowned. "I hadn't thought of that. Is it important?"

"Oh, yeah. If you want to be taken seriously, you've got to flash the diamond."

"We'll make an excuse." She didn't really expect this investigation to take more than a couple of days, certainly not long enough that she'd need to worry about a real diamond engagement ring.

Pacing around the conference table, she pointed to a door at the rear. "What's back there?"

"Files and my own private office where I can put my feet up on the desk and scratch my belly."

"So you start your couples in the classy reception area up front, then you bring them in here to do the actual planning. And behind door number three is where the real work takes place."

"You got it." He nodded. "What do you need to get started?"

Though she'd never done a field investigation of her own, Molly knew how to gather information and deduce patterns. "I want your files on each wedding where there's been a theft."

"Okay," he said. "Why?"

"Your magpie thief knows where the weddings will take place, and he knows the schedule. Therefore, we'll start with the assumption that this is an inside job."

"Are you saying that the magpie is somebody I know?"

"Well, yeah. That's the definition of an inside job." When did Pierce Williams get to be so naive? "After I go through your files, I'll know who worked on all the weddings where there were thefts. That's a start."

A grin lifted his heavy features. "You sound like you know what you're doing with this investigating stuff."

"You bet I do." She confidently tossed her hair.

"You remind me of Erin Brockovich."

"Yeah?" She adjusted the silver concha belt on her denim miniskirt. "You think I have the smarts of Erin Brockovich? Or the cleavage?"

"Both," he said.

She followed Pierce into his back office where a plain Formica-topped desk and computer station stood in front of several file cabinets.

"All the paperwork is in the files," he said. "But your search might be quicker on the computer."

She planted herself in the chair behind the desk and fired up the flat-screen monitor. "Nice equipment."

"I got a deal," he said.

"I've been telling Adam for months that we need to update our computer system. If I left things up to him, we'd be using homing pigeons for mail and doing accounts on an abacus."

Pierce leaned over the desk and punched a few computer keys, bringing up a document. "For somebody who doesn't have an interest in Adam, you talk about him a lot."

"We work together." She shrugged, not wanting to consider the state of her relationship with Adam too deeply. Right now, there wasn't much to consider in the way of any relationship with any man. Her dance card was a total blank; she hadn't been on a date in weeks. "Let's talk about you. How's your love life?"

"Still divorced and playing the field. In my job, I meet a lot of horny bridesmaids."

"That's sleazy, Pierce."

"It's not my fault if the ladies keep throwing themselves in my path."

Molly had to wonder if one of those ladies might be the thief. A woman scorned might try a couple of petty thefts to get his attention. "Do any of these ladies hold a grudge?"

"Not that I'm aware of."

"What about employees? Do you have anybody who works for you?"

"Right now, I'm using part-time receptionists from a temp service. My full-time assistant is off having a baby and won't be back for a couple more weeks."

"So, she's not a suspect," Molly said. The idea of a pregnant cat burglar was too bizarre.

He pointed at the computer monitor. "Here's a list of what was taken. The notation on the side tells which wedding."

Pierce had been accurate when he said that none of the stolen items were valuable. Nothing on this list was worth more than a hundred bucks. There were several kitchen appliances: a toaster, a Cuisinart, a coffeemaker.

Molly brushed him away. "Leave me alone with these files. I'll see what I come up with."

After a couple of hours combing through his files, she had a new respect for her friend's organizational skills. Planning a high-end wedding seemed nearly as complicated as invading a small country. There were caterers, wedding cake bakers, society page reporters, wine merchants, videographers, musicians, florists and couturiers to coordinate.

In the five weddings where there had been a burglary,

three names came up consistently: a caterer, a photographer and the woman who provided the gowns for the bridal party. Those were her suspects, and she needed to meet them face-to-face.

Molly entered the inner office where Pierce was on the phone. With calendars for sporting events tacked on the walls and a minibasketball hoop over the wastebasket, the decor was more suitable for a locker room than a wedding planner's office.

When he was off the phone, Molly announced the three names of her primary suspects. She started with, "Ronald Atchison, the photographer. I know Ronald, so I'll call him and set up a meeting."

Pierce nodded. "Who else?"

"Denny Devlin, the caterer. Wasn't there a scandal about him?"

"It's a sad story. Last year, one of his employees was discovered to have hepatitis. Everybody who attended Devlin's catered events had to get vaccinations. That incident damn near put him out of business."

"But you continue to use him."

"Because he's the best." Pierce pitched a crumpled-up wad of paper through the basketball hoop and into the wastebasket. "I've even loaned him money to keep going. Are you sure we need to suspect him?"

"Yes," Molly said. "Make an appointment for me to meet him."

"And who's suspect number three?"

"Gloria," she said.

Gloria Vanderly, the couturier for bridal gowns and bridesmaids' dresses, had a stellar reputation. She dealt with the top designers in New York, Paris and Milan. She was also Pierce's ex-wife.

"No way," Pierce said.

"She's been at all the weddings," Molly said.

"Think about it, Molly. You've met Gloria, and she's designer chic from her eyebrows to her toenail polish, which I happen to know costs twenty-five bucks a bottle. Gloria doesn't even know how to use a toaster, much less how to steal one."

"Maybe that's what she wants you to think." Molly posed a different theory. "Maybe Gloria is stealing this little stuff to cause you embarrassment. Or for revenge."

"Our divorce was real civilized, and we still work together. Her shop is right next door."

"Convenient," Molly said. "Let's pay Gloria a visit so I can scratch her name off the list of suspects."

After Pierce transferred all calls to his cell phone, they exited through the front door of his office and strolled a few paces on the sidewalk to the entrance for Vanderly's Bridal Boutique.

It was hard to imagine a divorce so friendly that the husband and wife still maintained close professional connections, and Molly thought Pierce might not be seeing the whole picture. His ex-wife wouldn't want to destroy him because that would hurt her own business, but she might take devious pleasure in watching him squirm.

The boutique's display window showed a mannequin in a bridal gown, with a front panel of exquisite lace, fit for a princess. Inside the boutique, a plush rose carpet cushioned their footsteps. There was a subtle undercurrent of classical music. And a fragrance. Lilac?

An attractive young receptionist sat at an antique white desk. She fluttered her eyelashes at Pierce who was, after all, a very eligible bachelor. Before she could speak, Gloria herself came into the reception area. She was a tall woman, nearly six feet, and reed thin in her black jersey top and capri-length slacks. Her shining black hair was clipped in a classic, chin-length bob.

In one glance, she assessed Molly from head to toe. Her eyelids blinked twice. *Ka-ching. Ka-ching.* And Molly knew that her total assets had been tallied and found wanting.

Gloria asked, "Have we met?"

"Once before. I'm Molly Griffith." She stuck out her hand. "I'm an old friend of Pierce's. That's why I wanted him as my wedding planner when I got engaged."

Gloria's manicured handshake was surprisingly strong. "No engagement ring?"

"It's being sized," Molly said. "I'll be doing all the wedding planning myself because my fiancé is out of town."

"And what's his name?" Gloria inquired.

"Rafael DuBois."

"His business?"

"He runs a multimillion dollar ranch." Molly felt as if she were taking a liar's quiz. She really hadn't figured out all the details of her cover story.

"A ranch in Colorado?"

"In Australia."

"What sort of ranch?" Gloria asked.

"Kangaroos." Molly said.

Pierce stepped forward. "Her future husband is rich, so Molly will spare no expense."

"Will the wedding be here in Denver?" Gloria asked.

"Right," Molly said. "Where else?"

"With your little miniskirt and the leopard collar, I assumed you might be more at home in Vegas. At the Little Chapel of Elvis." She tempered the insult with a well-bred ha-ha-ha. "I'm joking, of course."

Molly echoed the fake laugh. Gloria had thrown her off guard, but she wasn't about to lie down and let this snooty woman insult her. Time to unsheath the claws. Molly gave Gloria's slim outfit a glance and said, "I find basic black to be so dull. So trite. So totally last season."

"My dear, black is always classic."

"Exactly," Molly said. "Classic as in…old."

"Ladies, excuse me," Pierce said as he retreated into the showroom. He stood outside the curtain separating the fitting room. "Heidi? Are you in there?"

A small voice wailed, "Pierce! Come in here. I need your opinion."

When he pulled aside the curtain, Molly and Gloria followed him into the large mirrored room where a fitting was under way. The petite bride fidgeted on a raised pedestal. The tailor was on his knees, pinning her hem.

As Pierce offered a series of appropriate compliments to the bride, Molly realized why the former Bronco did so well in this unremittingly feminine business. He had a gift for making women feel attractive without being gushy.

Molly thought guys like Adam would do well to take lessons from Pierce, who was quick to flatter but didn't stoop to lying.

He pointed the petite bride toward the back wall where she was reflected in three mirrors. Pierce gave instructions to the tailor, "Be sure the skirt is high enough to show off her slim ankles and her tiny little feet."

"Ignore him," Gloria said. "The design of this gown is to the floor."

"Pierce might be right," the bride said. "We could bring up the hem in the front and leave the train in the back."

"That wasn't the intention." Gloria's smile was rigid. "The extra length of the hem will elongate your height and—"

"I want my shoes to show."

"Excuse me for a moment," Gloria said.

She took Molly by the arm and escorted her toward an array of design books, magazines and sample gowns displayed on padded hangers. "I'll have to leave you alone for a moment, Molly. Feel free to browse so we can get an idea of your style."

"I guess Pierce is causing trouble for you," Molly said.

"He always does."

"You're very understanding. Not many women would be able to work with an ex-husband."

There was a tightness around Gloria's perfectly made-up eyes. "I've found that Pierce is a far better business associate than a spouse."

Before Gloria turned away, Molly asked, "If I see something I like, can I try it on?"

Gloria snapped her fingers, and the tailor joined them. "This is Stan Lansky. He'll assist if you find a dress you'd like to try."

Gloria pivoted and returned to the opposite side of the shop where Pierce and the bride were chatting and laughing. She pulled the curtain closed around them.

In the midst of all this high-class couture, Stan Lansky was a dose of reality. As plain as his name, he was a bland, rabbity little man with a thin-lipped smile.

"Hi, Stan." When Molly shook his hand, he seemed surprised. "How do you like working for Gloria?"

"Very much, indeed." He had a slight European accent. "Gloria has remarkable taste."

Molly noticed that Stan didn't say *good* taste. "Are you a designer?"

"I've tried my hand." He nodded like a bobble-head doll.

Trying to place his accent, she guessed, "Did you study design in Paris?"

"In Brooklyn. My father was a tailor. From Prague."

Molly stroked the folds of a strapless gown of flowing satin. Though she was supposed to be investigating, the wedding finery was casting a spell over her. She was captivated by a long-sleeved gown with a plunging neckline. "This is nice."

"A good choice," Stan said.

"What if I wanted to try this on?"

"Our best gowns are one of a kind. But I can check in the back room to see if we have something similar in your size."

"In the back room?" She assumed that Gloria's boutique, though several times larger than Pierce's office, had a similar floor plan, with a reception area in front and the real offices in the rear. It might be useful to get a look behind the scenes.

She strode past the changing rooms. "Let's go."

Stan raced to catch up with her. "I'm sorry, miss. I really shouldn't allow you to—"

Molly found the door leading to the rear and pushed it open. The store room was scrupulously clean, carpeted and well-lit with racks of gowns stored in plastic dry cleaner's bags. There was also a cutting table, rolls of fabric, hatboxes, shoe boxes and sewing supplies.

"Do you work back here?" she asked Stan.

"Mostly. Miss, I insist. You must come back out front with me."

"How does this work?" She went to the rear door. "You order the gowns, and they're shipped here."

"Then we have at least two fittings." He darted a

glance at the door and wrung his small hands. "Gloria won't be happy if she finds you here."

But Molly wasn't working for Gloria. She was working for Pierce, and his ex-wife was a suspect, which meant poking around in all the dark corners. As Molly checked out the break room, she wondered if the coffeepot was new. Or stolen.

Returning to the center of the room, she handled the fabric of a gown that was laid out on the cutting table.

Stan groaned. "Don't touch."

She noticed a few loose threads at the neckline. "This one looks like it needs some work."

Gloria burst into the room. "Stan! What the hell is she doing back here?"

"Not his fault," Molly said. "I wanted to take a look around. This is really quite an operation. How many weddings do you handle at one time?"

"Several," she hissed.

"Just look at all these rich fabrics and sequins and lace." She meandered around the work table. "You don't have much security back here. Do you worry about theft?"

"My security system is sufficient."

"How so?" Molly looked her straight in the eye. In her high-heeled boots, she was as tall as Gloria. "Do you have a guard dog? A big old mastiff?"

"Certainly not."

"If I were you, I'd think about getting one. Or maybe you need a gun. Do you have a gun?"

"Let's get one thing straight, Molly. I will be delighted to assist you in planning couture for your wedding. But my business is strictly private."

"I like to know how things work."

"You're quite an unusual customer," Gloria said

stiffly. "Most brides are content to believe that their gowns appear magically, as if delivered by winged fairies."

"I'm not most brides."

"I should say not." Gloria looked down her nose. "An absent fiancé. No ring. And, from what I can see, no taste."

"Excuse me?"

"You heard me," Gloria said with a sneer. "Let's be realistic, Molly. There's no way you can afford to be in this boutique. Go back to the bargain basement where you belong and stop wasting my time."

Pierce barged into the back room. "Hey, Molly. What are you doing here?"

"I was looking for a dress to try on."

Stan raced up to her with a dress encased in plastic. "Here it is."

Together, she and Pierce walked past Gloria, whose attitude was chillier than the iceberg that sank the *Titanic*.

Drop dead, Gloria. After her comment about the bargain basement, Molly sure as hell was going to try this dress on. Maybe even rip out a seam or smear lipstick on the hem.

As soon as the silky fabric touched her skin, she knew it would be sacrilege to harm this gown. This was the true definition of luxury. The tiny buttons on the long sleeves fascinated her. The weight of the gown felt substantial, yet the supple skirt whispered around her legs as she emerged from the dressing room and went to stand in front of the mirror. Her skin glowed against the creamy white of the gown, and she felt amazing.

"You look beautiful," Pierce said.

This might be as close as Molly would ever come to

being a real bride. She was thirty-three with no special prospects. Though she had been married briefly to a scumbag when she was eighteen, she'd never honestly been in love.

A wistful sigh pushed through her lips. Being an undercover bride was a little depressing.

Chapter Three

Driving west toward Golden, Molly squinted into the midafternoon sun. Until a few hours ago, her unmarried status hadn't seemed like a big deal. She was an independent woman with a job, a car and a mortgage. Why did she need a man? Or a marriage?

Then, she tried on that gown and looked into a mirror that reflected the image of herself as a bride. Strange yearnings welled up inside her, washing away her defenses and leaving her vulnerable. She felt the weight of regret in a torrent of unshed tears, and she heard the unsung music of laughter she had never shared. Somewhere in the most secret recesses of her heart, she wanted to be a bride dressed in white—cherished and beloved. She wanted the ceremony and the gifts and the pledge of everlasting love in a glowing relationship.

Unfortunately, being a bride meant she needed a groom, and she had no clue to his identity.

Molly exited the highway and slowed as she drove into Golden. She hadn't accomplished very much in the way of investigation today. Sure, she'd narrowed the field of suspects to three, but she had no idea how to ferret out the evidence. All she'd learned in her meeting with Gloria was that they hated each other.

She had to do better with the others.

Ronald Atchison, the wedding photographer, would meet with her tomorrow. And Pierce had arranged an appointment with Denny Devlin, the caterer, at six o'clock this evening.

In the meantime, she had another problem to handle. If she intended to pass herself off as a bride-to-be, she needed a suitably flashy engagement ring. When she'd talked to Ronald, he was thrilled about her supposed engagement and couldn't wait to ogle the diamond.

Which was why she was on her way back to the CCC offices. At her desk, she had the addresses and phone numbers for a couple of jewelers who had done volunteer work for CCC involving jewel heists. She could borrow a ring from one of them.

Behind the office, she zipped into her parking place beside Adam's Land Cruiser. Though it was after four o'clock, he was still here. Damn. She wasn't looking forward to another conversation with him.

If this were a regular CCC investigation, she and Adam would share information and develop their ideas as a team. But this case was different. Molly had something to prove that had nothing to do with Pierce's petty thefts. She wanted to show Adam that she was competent and worthy of his respect—not only as an administrator, but as a detective. Her goal was to become partner and ultimately to hire someone else to do the administrative work.

When she pushed open the door to the CCC office, she was greeted by utter silence. The cluttered surface of her desk showed that Adam had tried to navigate his way through her filing system. The In box held the day's worth of mail with a stuffed pink teddy bear perched on top.

She remembered that Adam's two-year-old niece was here. Had he taken the child for a walk? It didn't seem likely that he'd leave the front door to the office unlocked.

The door to his inner sanctum was ajar, and she peeked inside. There he was. Sound asleep on the sofa. On his lap, he held Amelia, also napping.

The two of them made an adorable picture. The little girl's rosy cheek rested against Adam's starched white shirt front. Her blond curls tickled just under his chin. Though he held the child protectively, there was nothing of the hard-edged Marine about him. The lines at his mouth and eyes were smooth. His hair was mussed. He looked paternal and almost sweet.

Molly fought the urge to tiptoe toward them and place a small kiss on both their foreheads.

Adam's blue eyes opened. As he looked at Molly, he placed his finger across his lips, signaling silence. Carefully, he lifted Amelia off his chest and stretched her out on the sofa. After a few wiggles, the little girl went back to sleep.

Adam crept from the room and closed the door. He whispered, "I don't want to wake her. The kid's been on fire all day."

"Toddlers are a handful." She regarded him warily as he raked a hand through his neatly barbered dark blond hair, sweeping it back off his forehead. She asked, "How was your day?"

"Fine." He focused on her. "What about you? How's your investigation?"

Their questions seemed overly formal and polite. There was a distance between them, and she didn't like it one bit. Circling her desk, she sat in the swivel chair. "You're not still angry, are you? About my decision to investigate?"

"You're the one who left in a huff this morning."

"It wasn't a *real* huff," she said. "When I'm really mad, I throw things. There's blood."

He leaned across her desk and stared directly into her face. "I need to tell you something, Molly."

His tone was serious, which was not a good thing. She much preferred their usual bickering, which was always done with genuine affection. "I'm ready."

"It seems that I don't tell you often enough that I appreciate you."

"Okay." She eyed him curiously. Was he trying to be nice?

"Consider yourself told." He stood up straight. "And I am very interested in your investigation. Tell me what you've found out. I might be able to help."

"Don't you think I can figure it out on my own?"

"Far from it." His voice was low, trying not to wake his sleeping niece. "I have complete faith in your abilities."

She was taken aback. "You do?"

He held up two fingers. "That would be twice I've complimented you. Ready for another?"

"Go for it."

"While you were gone today, I realized something." He pointed to the clutter scattered across her desktop. "I couldn't find anything. There were file photos I needed from a crime scene, and I didn't know where to look. Couldn't locate the proper phone numbers. I spent half an hour searching for the scissors."

"I've shown you the filing system before," she said. "It's alphabetical and cross-referenced. A chimp could figure it out."

"When it comes to computers, I'm not a talented primate." Adam was accustomed to tossing out a single reference and having her respond with every bit of information he needed and more. "Things aren't right when you're not here."

He realized that efficiency wasn't really what he was talking about. He'd missed her in a more visceral sense. He'd been lonely without her, wanted to talk to her, wanted to see her sitting behind the desk. When she was gone, it felt as if he were missing half of his brain. "So. Tell me about your investigation."

"I reviewed the files for the weddings where items were stolen and came up with three suspects. I met with one—a couturier."

"A what?"

"Someone who provides wedding gowns and bridesmaid dresses. I tried one on."

Adam cocked his head to one side, trying to imagine Molly in a wedding dress. It was a stretch. He couldn't remember ever seeing her without splashy color and bangles. "Other suspects?"

"A photographer. And a caterer. I'm going back into town to meet with the caterer in about an hour. But I needed something from the office."

"What's that?"

She raised her left hand. "I can't pass myself off as an undercover bride without an engagement ring. I thought I could contact that jeweler we worked with and borrow one."

"Not necessary," he said. "I have a ring."

Her eyes widened in surprise. Adam had never before noticed that her irises were a remarkable shade of blue. Of course, he knew her eyes were pretty, but today the color shone with a breathtaking luster.

He forced himself to look away. This was Molly he was ogling—not some abstract woman that he might consider dating. Molly was his friend, his assistant, the woman he'd pulled from a life of crime and…

"Where's this ring, Adam?"

"In the safe."

He strode to the conference room adjoining the main office. On the far wall, he removed a framed aerial photograph of the Aspen area to reveal the tumblers of a fireproof titanium wall safe. It was hardly ever used, and he'd taken to keeping his personal papers and valuables here rather than at his home.

"This is my mother's engagement ring." He reached up to spin the numbered dial on the safe. "Not an antique, but it's very valuable."

Molly placed her hand on his forearm, stopping him. She stood close beside him—so close that he could smell the sweet floral scent of her perfume. "Adam, I don't feel right about using your mother's ring."

"Why not?"

"I don't want to take the chance that I might lose it. The ring is important to you."

"I'm not sentimental." He removed her hand and turned his attention to the safe that was cemented into the outer wall of the house. "It's less complicated for you to wear this ring than to track down something through a jeweler."

She stepped back. "Thank you."

Besides, he wanted to help her in this investigation. This ring was irrefutable, tangible evidence that he supported her and believed in her abilities. "It's a perfect diamond. I suppose that's suitable for your made-up fiancé."

"Rafael DuBois," she said.

He snorted. "Fancy name."

"He's a fancy fantasy guy," she said. "Fabulously wealthy. And handsome."

"His profession?"

"He's from Australia. And he has a ranch where he raises…kangaroos."

"A highly profitable endeavor," Adam said.

"I've only seen you open that safe once or twice before," she said. "What have you got in there?"

"Deeds. Some cash. Medals." He had two Purple Hearts. "I have a handgun in here. You might consider carrying a weapon while you're investigating."

She shook her head. "Don't need it."

"You're sure?"

"This isn't what I'd call a dangerous crime. Also, I don't want to bother with the paperwork for a license to carry a concealed weapon."

The safe opened. He fished around inside until he touched the velvet-covered box that held his mother's engagement ring.

As Adam opened the small box to show Molly, a sense of irony crept over him. This ring should have signaled the eternal bond of love between himself and the woman he would marry. Instead, he was giving it to Molly to use on a criminal case.

Perhaps his dedicated fight against crime was his real life partner. Not a woman. Not hearth and home. Perhaps Adam was married to his work.

Until this moment, that had seemed like enough. Now, he had a sense of wanting more.

"It's exquisite," Molly said as she beheld the square-cut center stone flanked by two smaller diamonds on a platinum band. "And very impressive. Three diamonds."

"My mother said the three gems symbolized a brilliant past, present and future. My parents were married for forty-five years. They died within a month of each other."

"Adam, this ring is precious to you. I don't think I should—"

"I want you to have it."

He grasped her left hand and slid the ring onto her finger. It was a perfect fit.

Though he should have been pledging his undying love with this ring, the fact that Molly was wearing it felt somehow right.

She held the ring up to the light, admiring the sparkle from the faceted diamonds. When she smiled, her face glowed. Her cheeks warmed. Had her complexion always been so flawless? She looked younger now than on the day they had met seven years ago. "Thank you, Adam."

He cleared his throat. Gruffly, he said, "I'll do anything to get you through this investigation and back at your desk as quickly as possible."

"Of course," she said. "This is a smart, efficient business strategy."

And yet, when he looked into her eyes, he saw a longing as if she wanted to kiss him.

A similar urge rose within him, and he turned away from her. There were rules Adam lived by, and one of the most basic was: no personal relationships in the workplace. He'd be a fool to get involved with Molly. If it didn't work out, he'd lose the best assistant he ever had.

Calling upon his prodigious self-control, he closed the safe and turned back toward her. "Good luck in your investigation."

A sly smile lifted the corners of her mouth. "I appreciate your support. You're not as much of a tightass as I thought you were."

"The so-called tightness of my ass has nothing to do with my need to—"

"I know," she said. "You want me back here to make your coffee and keep your files. Don't worry. This should only take a day or two."

He hoped she was right.

BY THE TIME Molly reached Pierce's office at a few minutes until six, it was already dark. The evening breeze held the snap of autumn, a portent of the winter snows. But she wasn't at all cold. Ever since Adam's ring encircled her finger, Molly felt a warmth that radiated from within.

Though she was well aware that this engagement ring was nothing more than an undercover disguise, it made her feel special to be wearing it. This beautiful diamond opened the door to an elite club of women who were beloved, engaged to be married. And it didn't bother her too much that she was engaged under false pretenses. She'd crashed a lot of parties in her day.

Parked beside the Dumpster at the rear of Pierce's shop, she paused for a moment and held up her hand. The brilliant gems shimmered in the light of a streetlamp, as though a star had fallen from the heavens and come to rest on her hand. Pretending to be engaged was so amazing that she could hardly imagine the real thing—especially since her one and only marriage wasn't an experience she wanted to repeat.

She left her car and went to the rear door of Pierce's office. It was unlocked. She slipped inside and called out, "I'm here. Pierce?"

Her voice echoed, but there was no answer.

The lights in the back area were on, and she peered into his office. Nobody there.

A shadow of foreboding crept over her.

She opened the door leading into the middle section

of his office with the conference table and the bridal catalogs. In here, the overhead lights were dark, and the only illumination came from the other side of the partition in the front office and reception area.

Molly had never liked the dark. From the time she was a little girl, she imagined monsters under the bed. She felt at the wall for a light switch but couldn't find one.

"Pierce?" A shiver ricocheted inside her rib cage, and her heart beat faster. Tension prickled the hairs on her arms as she edged carefully toward the partition.

Her fingers tightened into fists. For a moment, she thought about the gun from Adam's safe. She should have taken it.

Light from the street spilled through the front window and highlighted the classy sofa and chairs. A small lamp cast an amber glow on the desktop.

On the beige carpet, she saw Pierce. He lay face-down. A knife handle protruded from the center of his back.

Molly raced toward him and fell to her knees beside him. My God, this couldn't be happening! She was investigating a petty theft, searching for a magpie. Not a murderer.

She touched Pierce's hand. It was warm.

When she felt for a pulse at his wrist, he moved. He was still alive.

Chapter Four

It was up to Molly to save Pierce's life. She knew the rudiments of first aid. Adam had taught her. But what came first in first aid? She couldn't think!

Frantically, she ripped open her purse and pulled out the cell phone. She speed-dialed Adam.

As soon as he answered, she said, "It's Pierce. He's been stabbed."

"Where are you?" Adam asked.

"His shop." She recited the address. "He's alive. How do I stop the bleeding?"

"Have you called 911?"

That should have been her first response. She should have known. "No."

"Is the attacker still there?"

Her gaze flitted from shadow to shadow in the dimly lit room. *Was he still here?* She hadn't thought of danger to herself. When she saw Pierce, her concern for him blanked out everything else. "I don't know if he's here."

"Get out of there," Adam said. "Now."

But if she ran, the assassin might return to finish the job. "I won't leave Pierce."

"Stay on the phone," Adam ordered. "I'll use the other line to call for an ambulance."

She gripped the outflung hand of her wounded friend and squeezed his fingers. The diamonds in her borrowed engagement ring twinkled ironically in the light from the window. Moments ago, she'd been almost happy.

Leaning over Pierce, she whispered, "Help is on the way. You're going to be all right."

He made no sound. His body was still. His life force was slipping away. She could almost hear the slowing of his heartbeat.

"Pierce," she called desperately to him. "Stay with me."

It seemed impossible that he would die. He was such a big, muscular man. Full of strength. Full of life. How had anyone gotten close enough to attack him?

"Molly." She heard Adam's voice on the phone. "Are you there?"

"What can I do for him?"

"Don't try to remove the knife. You might cause further bleeding." Adam's voice was calm. "I've called an ambulance. The paramedics will be there. Let them handle—"

"There has to be something I can do."

"If you can find a blanket, cover him."

A blanket. She thought of the center room with all the bridal supplies. There might be something there. "I'll look."

She gave one more squeeze to Pierce's limp hand and bolted upright. As she stood, too quickly, the sheer horror of the situation crashed around her. Her legs were unsteady. Fighting dizziness, she stood very still, regaining her wits and her balance. The last thing she needed right now was to pass out. A fainting spell? No way. She wasn't that type of woman. Not a delicate flower. Molly was tough. She was a weed.

Over the cell phone, Adam said, "Tell me what you're doing."

"I'm going to the center room." The faint light in the room was disorienting. When she took a step, she couldn't feel her feet. "There's only one lamp. It's dark in here."

Squinting, she spied a light switch near the front entrance. "First, I'll turn on the overhead lights."

Walking carefully, she reached the front door and flipped the switch. Nothing happened.

"Did you find the lights?" Adam asked.

"They don't work. Must be a blown fuse."

"Are you near an exit?"

"Yes."

"Open the door," Adam said. "Call for someone to help you."

A very smart idea! She twisted the knob and pulled. The carved oak door remained closed. "There's a dead bolt."

"How did you get in?"

"Through the rear."

"Go back that way," Adam said.

She peered into the shadows in the office. Behind the separating partition was total dark. Was someone there? The air seemed to move, gradually taking form then dissipating in foul miasma.

Tension pumped adrenaline through her system. No way would she walk through those thick, looming shadows. "It's too dark. I can't go back that way."

"Keep talking to me," Adam said.

Her heart raced. She was literally trembling with fear. Her instincts told her to hide, to seek cover. But she'd never been a coward.

"Molly!" Adam's voice snapped through the cell phone.

Her irritation was automatic. She snapped, "What?"

"You need to find the key. So you can open the door for the paramedics. Talk to me, Molly."

She gripped the cell phone, white-knuckled. It was her lifeline. She forced herself to take a step. "I'll look in the desk. Maybe there are keys in the drawer."

But the desk was locked. Pierce must have the keys. They must be in his pocket.

"Now I'm going back toward Pierce. He's not moving, Adam."

"You've got to open that door."

Crouched down, she searched Pierce's trouser pockets. "His wallet is in his back pocket. I can't find the damn keys."

She forced her hand under him, shifting his considerable weight to search both front pockets. Her fingers closed around the key ring. "Got it."

From the rear of the offices, she heard a clatter. The noise went through her like a shock wave and she gasped. "Adam, somebody's in here."

Holding her breath, she waited for the darkness to take form and charge like the monsters that lived under her bed when she was a little girl. *Where was the ambulance? Why were they taking so long?*

"Calm down, Molly. Take the keys and go to the door."

But if she stood at the door, she'd be exposed. Instead, she crawled across the carpet to the beige sofa, chairs and coffee table. She stayed low, hiding from the faint light that spilled through the front window, wishing she could be invisible.

"Molly, talk to me."

"I don't know what to do." She was scared, and she hated the fear. The helplessness. Molly was big and brash. She could handle anything. And yet, she was cowering.

"Find a weapon," Adam said.

"What?" She glared at the cell phone. "This is a wedding planner's office. Not an armory."

"There must be something."

"A lamp." Clumsily, she reached up and grasped the neck of a table lamp. She yanked the cord from the wall and stood. "I can use this as a club."

"Do you see anyone?"

"No."

"Open the damn door."

"Easy for you to say." His total lack of empathy ticked her off. "You're not trapped in a beige office with a dying man."

"I wish it was me instead of you," Adam said. "But it's not. Pull yourself together, Molly."

He was always giving orders. Even now when she might be in mortal danger, Adam wouldn't cut her any slack. Her anger at him gave her a surge of energy. "All right. I'm going to the door."

Gripping the heavy lamp, she stalked across the carpet toward the door. She had to set down her weapon to flip through the keys on the ring. Her fingers were shaky, and that sign of weakness irritated her even more.

The overhead lights came on. The sudden flash blinded her.

Molly whirled, dropping the cell phone. The sight of Pierce's body—fiercely illuminated—shocked her. Crimson streaks of blood stained the beige carpet. The back of his shirt was dark red. She saw another wound on his skull. A bit of white fabric lay beside him. A bride's veil.

How the hell could this have happened? It was

wrong. She grabbed the lamp and brandished it like a baseball bat. "You want a fight?"

She braced herself against the door. Nobody was going to attack her from behind. "Bring it on."

More than bravado, this was rage—a huge, powerful burst of anger that eclipsed her terror. She was ready to attack.

The screech of an ambulance siren cut through the night. Finally!

Molly turned her attention to the door. She found the key, unlatched the dead bolt and flung it open.

A cool evening breeze gushed against her hot cheeks and forehead. She caught a gulp of the fresh air. Her sense of relief was huge, as if she'd escaped from the depths of a drowning pool.

Keeping the door ajar, she picked up the cell phone. The blare of the ambulance siren serenaded her. The flashing lights of the emergency vehicle were beautiful.

To Adam, she said, "The paramedics are here. I'll call you from the hospital."

Gratefully, she stepped aside as the paramedics did their job.

"He's alive," she told them.

"Yes, ma'am. We'll take it from here."

Molly turned away from the sight of her injured friend. Though she was still wary, the tension drained from her as reality soaked in.

The simple fact was this: someone had tried to kill Pierce. She couldn't believe he'd been attacked because of a few stolen appliances. Apparently, she was investigating something more than petty theft. Much bigger.

She stood in the doorway. On the sidewalk outside

the office, a small crowd had gathered. The people in a Starbucks across the four-way-stop intersection craned their necks.

From the office next door, Gloria and the tailor, Stan Lansky, appeared.

"What's going on?" Gloria demanded.

"It's Pierce." Molly was glad that she'd recovered enough of her poise to face this witch without trembling. "He's been injured."

"Injured in what way?" Gloria tossed her head, sending a ripple through her shining black hair. She didn't seem very concerned about her ex-husband.

The paramedics emerged from the office, carrying Pierce on a stretcher that they loaded quickly into the ambulance.

Gloria came closer. Her lips were tight. Her expression unreadable.

"He was stabbed," Molly said. "In the back."

Gloria looked past her into Pierce's office. She strode inside. With two fingers, she plucked a scrap of blood-stained netting and ribbons from the floor. "It looks like I'll need to order a new veil."

WITH HIS NIECE loaded in her car seat, Adam drove to the Denver Medical Center, where Pierce had been taken. He was plenty mad at Molly for getting herself enmeshed in a dangerous investigation. She'd blithely walked into a crime scene. She could have been injured. She could have been killed.

While he talked to her on the phone, not knowing if she'd live or die, he'd been in his own special hell. Many times before, he'd been in situations where he saw danger approaching and was powerless to stop it. When he was in the Corps, he'd lost two men in his platoon. One to a sniper. One in a mine field. Their safety was his responsibility, and he had failed them. Thank God, Molly was all right.

From the backseat, Amelia babbled cheerfully. "Aunt Molly," she said. "We go see Aunt Molly."

"That's right, Amelia."

"Molly's pretty."

"Yes, she is," Adam said. "Aunt Molly is also a damn troublemaker."

"Damn pretty."

Adam winced. He knew better than to swear around this little parrot.

"I'm damn pretty," Amelia said. Then she began making barking noises. "I'm a doggy."

"Not really," he said.

"Am too. Woof."

They'd had this discussion several times today— enough that Adam feared his niece had found her calling in life. And it was canine.

He should probably talk to his sister about her daughter's obsession, but then he might have to explain about how he spent half the day today pretending to be a mastiff while Amelia was a poodle.

He parked in the lot outside the hospital, lifted Amelia from her car seat and went inside.

Among several other people in the waiting room, Molly sat in a plastic chair. Her complexion was pale. Her thick blond hair, disheveled. The sleeves of her denim jacket were stained with dried blood, and there were smears on her legs. Above her head, a television screen showed a sitcom with canned laughter.

As soon as she saw him, she leapt to her feet and came toward him. They'd been in tense situations before, but the danger had never been so personal.

He sat Amelia down on a chair and held open his arms. Molly stepped into his embrace. She clung tightly to him. For once, she didn't have a smart-aleck comment.

Her body felt warm in contrast to the cool from outdoors, but she was the one who shivered. Though he shouldn't have been thinking of her as a woman, a sensual being, he couldn't help his natural reaction as her body rubbed against his.

When he patted her back, his hand molded her slender torso.

She leaned away from him and gazed up at him. In her eyes, he saw her inner torment. Fear and sorrow were written clearly across her lovely face.

He could have offered meaningless reassurance, but she'd know he was lying. After seven years together, they communicated silently at a deep level.

He asked, "Have you heard anything about Pierce?"

"He's in surgery," she said.

Amelia had scooted off the chair and attached herself to Molly's leg. "Aunt Molly. I want hugs."

Molly stepped away from Adam and lifted the little girl. "How's it going, kiddo?"

"Woof." Amelia beamed. "I'm a poodle."

"Well, of course you are."

"Uncle Adam says you're damn pretty."

Molly's eyebrows raised in surprise. "Uncle Adam should know better than to swear in front of a poodle."

She sat with Amelia on a chair and turned to Adam. "Pierce's situation is critical, but his chances for survival are good. He lost a lot of blood. Has a punctured lung. And a concussion."

He was surprised that she'd managed to glean so much information. Molly wasn't a relative of Pierce's, and the E.R. wasn't usually so forthcoming with their initial prognosis. "How did you find this out?"

"You remember Blair Weston, don't you?"

"Dr. Blair?" She worked as a medical examiner and often did forensic consulting for CCC—most recently, she'd worked on a serial killer case.

"I called her," Molly said. "She got the inside scoop."

He should have been annoyed that Molly used her CCC contacts to bypass regular hospital protocol, but Adam wasn't about to scold. She'd been through enough tonight.

Little Amelia turned Molly's head toward her. "Play dog with me. Uncle Adam plays dog with me."

"Does he?"

"He's a mass-ive," Amelia said seriously.

"A mastiff," Adam corrected. "I'm a mastiff."

Molly cast him a sidelong glance, then chuckled. When she laughed, the color seemed to rise in her cheeks. Her tension lessened.

Sheepishly, Adam smiled. He didn't mind looking silly if it gave Molly some relief.

"How long do we have to stay here?" he asked.

"I want to wait until Pierce is out of surgery," she said. "And I still need to talk to the cops."

For once, he resented the time-consuming official procedures. He wanted to take Molly home and tuck her safely into bed…figuratively speaking. He wouldn't actually enter her bedroom. In fact, he couldn't remember ever being inside the bedroom at her cottage-sized house in Golden. They'd had coffee in her kitchen. They'd watched a hockey game in her living room. But there had never been a reason for him to enter her bedroom. Not once in seven years.

From her purse, Molly produced a notebook and a

couple of pens for Amelia to play with. Then she turned back to Adam. "I feel like the attack on Pierce is somehow my fault."

He automatically shook his head. "Doubtful."

"It can't be a total coincidence. Just when I start poking around, looking into the magpie thefts, Pierce is attacked."

"But no one knew you were investigating."

"It's somehow connected."

He put two and two together. "You're not going to give up on this investigation, are you?"

"How can I? Pierce needs me more than ever."

Though his instincts told him that nothing good could come of this investigation, Adam knew better than to try to dissuade her. Nor could he stand by while Molly sashayed into danger in her high-heeled boots. Not after tonight.

He had no desire to relive the ineffectual helplessness he'd experienced when he thought she might be attacked. "I have only one thing to say about your plan to—"

"Don't forbid me," she warned. "I hate it when you get all military and authoritarian."

He held out his hand toward her. "Have we met? I'm Adam Briggs, your new partner."

"You'll work with me on this?" Her blue eyes sparkled with the vivacious energy he'd always taken for granted. "Do you think we can close the office?"

"Everything's under control." None of their other cases required immediate supervision. "Well, Molly. Are we partners?"

She grasped his hand warmly. "You're on."

A HOSPITAL WAS NO PLACE for a thief, but he had been drawn here. The thief leaned against a tall oak at the edge of a park opposite Denver Medical Center. He would go no deeper into the park; there was a high school nearby, which meant gangs of teenagers.

Motionless, he rested against the tree trunk, watching the ambulances come and go, discharging human cargo, human suffering and pain.

Inside those brick hospital walls, Pierce Williams might be dying. It would be better for everybody if he passed away without ever revealing the secret he had learned. He ought to die.

But Pierce might have a second chance. He was lucky. The big football player. The big star.

Big fool! The thief had known the secret for many, many days. No one actually bothered to tell him or confide in him. They didn't notice him, didn't pay him any attention. He was invisible.

But he listened and he overheard and he learned. There had to be a profit for him in this crime. Somehow, he would be paid for his stolen knowledge.

The thief looked up. The pattern of window lights from the hospital rooms began to dim as the patients went to sleep one by one. Some would recover. Some would die.

Lucky Pierce. His friend, Molly, had showed up in the nick of time and called an ambulance. She'd better watch out. She might be next.

Chapter Five

The next morning, after she'd arranged baby-sitting for Amelia, Molly and Adam were driving back into Denver in his Land Cruiser. Her plan of action was to pick up where she left off on her investigation yesterday. Last night, she and Pierce were supposed to meet with Denny Devlin, the caterer.

"Tell me again," Adam said. "Why is Devlin a suspect?"

"He catered all the weddings where there were thefts. I don't have anything else to go on."

"It's a starting point."

He gazed benevolently at the panorama of the city that spread before them, and Molly studied his familiar profile. There was something different about Adam this morning. It wasn't just that he'd offered to be her partner, although that statement was something of a shocker. *Her partner?* Implying that they were, in fact, equals? That was certainly different from his usual commanding officer attitude. But there was something else…something weird.

His craggy profile looked the same as always. Exactly the same. Adam never changed his haircut, always wore the same style in casual trousers—khaki today—and lightly starched, button-down collar shirts. Same aviator sunglasses. Same leather jacket. What was different?

"For breakfast this morning," she said. "What did you have?"

"Corn flakes and milk. OJ."

Same as always.

"Did Amelia have the same?"

"She wanted puppy chow, but I convinced her that corn flakes were the preferred food for poodles." Though he kept his eye on the merging highway traffic, he grinned.

Ah ha! Molly thought she might have the answer. When Adam was with little Amelia, his nurturing side came out. "You like having your niece around."

"I didn't enjoy baby-sitting when she was an infant," he admitted. "I always felt like I was going to drop her or something. But now? That little girl lights up the room."

"Do you ever think about having kids of your own?"

"Sure. I think about it."

"And?"

"You know the answer, Molly. I'm a forty-two-year-old bachelor, set in my ways. My life is good and productive exactly the way it is. I see no reason to change."

Absolute control was his motto. As always.

She leaned back in the passenger seat and stared straight ahead through the windshield as they exited the highway and continued east on Sixth Avenue through town. After all these years together, she ought to know that he'd never really change. With Adam, what you saw was what you got. No surprises.

Still, his readiness to accept her as a partner signaled a difference. Or did it? She was certain that his real motivation for wanting to work with her on this investigation was because he wanted her back in the CCC offices full-time, taking care of his needs.

Nonetheless, she wouldn't complain. It was reassuring to have a rugged former Marine at her side while she tried to figure out who had attacked Pierce.

Poor Pierce! His condition had been upgraded to serious, and he'd regained consciousness long enough to tell the police detective that he hadn't seen his attacker. His inability to provide an ID was unfortunate, but plausible. He was stabbed in the back, probably clunked on the head first.

"We can visit Pierce this afternoon," she said. "After we see Denny Devlin."

"Our investigation might be wrapped up by then," Adam said. "I think the caterer is our man."

"Wait a minute," she said. "Don't you always tell me to keep an open mind on investigations?"

"It's obvious," he said. "The knife used to stab Pierce was a high-carbon, stainless steel chef's knife from Germany. The kind of blade a caterer would use."

"How do you know that?"

"Detective Berringer told me."

"That pig?"

Gruffly, Adam said, "You know how I feel about denigrating the Denver PD."

"Most of the cops are princes," she said, "and I love working with them. But Berringer? He's a creep."

He was one of those guys who never looked her in the eye but spoke directly to her cleavage. Though she knew for a fact that he was married with two kids, Berringer had asked her out for drinks more than once. And he wasn't happy when she'd turned him down flat. She hated that he'd been the officer assigned to this case.

Adam said, "Berringer also told me that there were no fingerprints on the handle of the knife blade."

"Which means?"

"Could mean the attack was premeditated," Adam said. "The assailant thought far ahead enough to bring the knife. And he was careful about not leaving prints."

"Or it could mean the knife was handy and the assailant wore gloves," she said. "The real significance is that the police don't have any leads."

"Nothing at all." As they pulled up at a stoplight, Adam glanced toward her. "As you well know."

Last night, she'd endured a snotty lecture from Berringer about how her attempt to save Pierce had messed up the criminal forensics. But what was she supposed to do? Stand by and let Pierce bleed to death? "I think you're wrong about Denny Devlin."

"Why?"

"If he planned to attack Pierce, why would he use gourmet cutlery that would point directly to him?"

"Tell me what you know about him."

"About a year and a half ago, one of his employees had hepatitis. All the food this employee handled was infectious, which meant that everybody who attended Devlin's catered events had to get inoculated. It was a big scandal."

"I'm surprised he's still in business," Adam said. "Why does Pierce use him?"

"Because, apparently, Devlin is good at what he does. Also, Pierce is a very loyal guy."

Like her, Pierce knew that people sometimes made mistakes…even criminal mistakes. It didn't mean they were bad people.

"It can't be Devlin," she said more firmly. "He owes Pierce a debt of gratitude for the continued business. Why would Devlin stab the hand that feeds him?"

Adam parked outside a small building with an equally small but tasteful sign: Devlin Catering. "Is there anything else I should be aware of before we proceed?"

"We're undercover," she said. "I'm planning my wedding, and I'm engaged to Rafael DuBois."

"The kangaroo farmer," Adam said dryly. "And why am I coming with you?"

"You're the best man."

"Which means I know the imaginary Rafael." He shook his head. "Not a good plan."

"Well, you can't be my maid of honor." She chuckled. "Though you'd be just adorable in a pink organza gown with rosebuds in your hair and—"

He growled. "That's enough, Molly."

"Let's keep it simple. You're a friend, helping me decide what to do at my wedding."

The interior of Devlin Catering was very white and spotlessly clean. In her red leather pants and jacket, Molly felt like a poppy in a snowstorm.

Behind the long white counter, she saw an impressive array of stainless steel cooking equipment. The mouthwatering fragrance of fresh baked pastry hung in the air.

A slim man in a white chef's jacket and poufed hat came to the counter. "You must be Molly."

"Must be." He seemed familiar, but she couldn't quite place him. "Do I know you?"

"We've met." He jogged around the counter and vigorously pumped her hand. "It's okay if you don't remember. I'm not a memorable kind of guy." He turned to Adam. "And is this the groom?"

"No," Adam said quickly and vehemently. "I'm just a friend. Molly and I work together."

"So you're helping her decide a menu?"

"Absolutely," Molly said. "Adam's great with food. A total gourmet."

"Right," Adam muttered. "As long as it's meat and potatoes."

When Denny Devlin smiled, he twinkled as if he'd been coated with sugar sprinkles. An aura of pink-cheeked cheerfulness radiated from him. Surely this taller, leaner version of a cookie-baking elf couldn't have attacked Pierce with a high-carbon, stainless steel chef's knife.

Yet, when Molly looked more deeply into his eyes, which were beady and rather close together, she saw an edge. Quite possibly, Denny wasn't as tasty as he first appeared to be.

He escorted them to a white table near the front window. As soon as they were seated, he offered, "Can I get you something to drink? Espresso? Or herbal tea?"

"Water would be fine," Molly said.

He rattled off half a dozen brands of bottled water, and she selected. Denny disappeared behind the counter and emerged carrying a tray with blue glasses, a plate of crudités and a sampling of various dips.

"This one is clam," he said. "This is honey Dijon. And this is wasabi, which is, of course, hot."

Though Molly enjoyed being catered to, she was afraid that the food-tasting atmosphere wasn't conducive to asking probing questions about the attack on Pierce. Nor was her cover story. Brides—even undercover brides—weren't given to interrogation. It was all about them and their wedding. Absently, she dipped a tender baby carrot into the honey Dijon.

Denny sat at the end of the table and pulled off his

chef's hat to reveal short, curly brown hair. "Tell me what you have in mind for your wedding, Molly."

"I'm not sure where to begin," she said. "I was counting on Pierce to help me. It's so terrible what happened to him."

"Terrible." But Denny got right back to the subject of food. "How many people at the reception?"

"Three hundred and thirty," she said, picking a number out of the air. "Did you know Pierce was stabbed in the back? I found him in his office. Bleeding."

A shadow dimmed Denny's features, but he quickly smiled again. "Will this be a sit-down dinner?"

"I guess so," she said.

"And the date?"

"Next year. September fourteenth."

Adam glanced up sharply. The date she'd thrown out happened to be his birthday. "That's a good day."

"September weddings," Denny said, "are my favorite. Have you chosen the venue?"

Molly shook her head. How could she get their conversation focused on Pierce? Maybe if she pretended to be upset, Denny would comfort her. She fluttered her hand before her face. "I'm so devastated."

Beside her, Adam gave a disbelieving snort.

She ignored him and focused on Denny. "Pierce is such a terrific guy. You've known him a long time, haven't you?"

Denny's lips pursed as if he'd sucked on a lemon. "I owe Pierce a lot."

"How so?"

"He's always supported me." Denny took a bound notebook from a shelf and handed it to her. "These are sample menus. Why don't you look through them and see if there's anything that appeals."

"About Pierce—"

"Excuse me." He stood. "I need to take something out of the oven."

Frustrated, Molly frowned. It was hard to pull information out of someone without being obvious. She glanced toward Adam and said quietly, "He doesn't want to talk."

"Let me take a crack at him."

"What do you mean?"

"Good cop, bad cop," Adam said. "You just keep being sweet."

Denny returned to the table with several tiny chocolate cookies. "Help yourself."

Molly dug in. The first bite of the warm cookie melted on her tongue. "Delicious."

"The secret is French butter," Denny said.

Though she was aware that she was eating pure calories, Molly finished off her cookie and reached for another.

"Adam?" Denny said, nudging the plate toward him. "Go ahead."

"Not interested." His expression was hard-edged and combative. "I'm not sure I feel safe eating here."

"Why not?" Denny said.

"I didn't want Molly to hire you." Adam's voice was a low, hard rumble—subtle as a semitruck barreling down the highway. "Not after the hepatitis incident."

Denny stepped back from the table as if he'd been physically shoved. "I assure you, Adam, that I run the cleanest catering service in town. You can inspect my kitchen."

"What about your employees? Wasn't that your problem the first time around? You hired somebody who was infected."

"That'll never happen again."

"Certainly not," Molly said. She reached over and patted Denny's arm. "Come sit down with us. I had a question about these menus."

Warily, Denny took his seat. "Nobody works for me without a physical checkup at hiring. And follow-ups every three months. All my employees are bonded."

"Bonded?" Adam questioned. "They don't handle money, do they?"

"Sometimes we cater events in the homes of the wealthy," Denny said.

"You're concerned about theft." There was a harsh note of triumph in Adam's voice. "Pierce mentioned items going missing at some of the weddings you've catered."

"I don't know what you're talking about."

His words came too fast, as though he were prepared for this denial. Molly studied him in a new light. Was Denny Devlin the magpie?

"The thief could have been one of your employees." Adam turned up the pressure. "One of those low-wage servers or cooks. If your people are stealing, that would be the last straw for you. That would put you out of business for sure."

"I'd already be closed down if it weren't for Pierce and Gloria." Denny's complexion darkened as his anger grew. "They made me a loan—a substantial amount. Because they believe in me and my work."

"You're the best," Molly put in. "That's what I've always heard."

She was beginning to catch the rhythm of this good cop/bad cop thing. Adam would throw out a nasty jab, then she'd soothe Denny's feelings before he completely shut down and threw them out.

Slightly placated, he turned toward her. "You had some questions about the menu?"

"Just last weekend, I attended the wedding of Kate Carradine and Liam MacKenzie. They had these adorable little tarts."

"They wanted to use gooseberries because they're native to Colorado," he said. "They had several odd requests about the food. It was a challenge."

"You did beautifully," Molly said.

"Thank you for noticing," he said. "I worked my fingers to the bone and came up with several brand new recipes. Most people don't appreciate my efforts."

"I do," she assured him.

"Most people just toss back the food and wash it down with champagne. The only time I hear about it is when something's wrong."

Adam pounced again. "There was a theft at that wedding. Did you know about it?"

Denny leapt to his feet. "What's your problem, anyway?"

Moving slowly and deliberately, Adam pushed back his chair and stood. His shoulders straightened. He held Denny Devlin in a dark, steady gaze that clearly said, "Don't mess with me."

Though Molly worked with Adam every day and teased him constantly, she was impressed with his kick-ass posture. This ex-Marine looked as if he could take on a whole battalion of Denny Devlins without breaking a sweat.

Adam said, "Pierce was stabbed in the back with a chef's knife—a specialty blade. You have access to that kind of weapon."

"Are you accusing me?"

"Where were you last night?"

"Not that it's any of your damned business, but I was here. Waiting for Pierce and Molly."

"Alone?" Adam asked.

"As a matter of fact, yes. I was alone. And that's what I told the police when they came by this morning and requested an inventory of my cutlery."

He was a suspect! The police were looking at him. "Why?" Molly asked. "Why did the police come to you?"

"Because of the damned knife that your friend seems so interested in. It's an expensive blade, but not rare. And not mine!"

Molly rose to her feet and stood between the two men. "Denny, I'm so terribly sorry for the way this turned out. Perhaps it's best if I make another appointment with you."

"Don't bring him," Denny snapped.

"I won't." She aimed Adam toward the exit, waving goodbye as she went. "Lovely to meet you."

Without a word, she and Adam hurried across the parking lot and climbed into his car. As they drove away from Devlin Catering, Molly howled, "So cool! The good cop/bad cop thing was fantastic!"

"We did okay," Adam said.

"Are you kidding? We're good together. I mean, we're really good together."

When she first started talking with Devlin, fumbling around and making up details about her fictitious wedding, it didn't seem she'd get anywhere. With Adam's help, they discovered a lot.

She summarized, "We know that Denny got a substantial loan from Pierce and Gloria. The police consider him a suspect, but the knife isn't from his inventory."

"What else?" Adam asked.

"He uses French butter in his cookies?"

"What else?"

She didn't know what he was getting at. "He has a lot of hostility under the surface?"

"He was alone last night at the time of the attack," Adam said. "No alibi."

Chapter Six

While Molly negotiated at the nurses' station to arrange a brief visit with Pierce, Adam stood by silently with his arms folded across his chest. He hated hospitals—the faintly antiseptic smell, the squeak of sneakers on the tile floors, the rattling carts, the bland walls. Hospitals were for the wounded. A visit to the wards tasted like bitter failure in the back of his mouth. He was not a healer, but a warrior. Here lay fallen comrades that Adam had been unable to protect.

He watched an old woman being pushed toward the elevators in a wheelchair. Her gnarled fingers gripped the metal arms of the chair. Her faded eyes were wide and yet unseeing.

Adam turned away. He remembered when he was a boy and had visited his mother in her hospital bed. He remembered the bruises on her face, her slender arm in a white plaster cast. She shouldn't have been there, lying in a bed of pain. He should have saved her.

Purposefully, Adam shut down that memory center. He was here to help Molly and wouldn't allow himself to be distracted from that purpose.

She came toward him. "We have five minutes with Pierce."

"Swell."

As he trailed her down the corridor, Adam avoided glancing into the rooms by concentrating on Molly. Watching her made him smile. In her flashy red outfit, she didn't belong in a hospital setting. Her step was jaunty. Her butt swished back and forth in her tight leather pants. Her long blond hair rippled across her shoulders.

He had an urge to touch her hair. If he reached out, he might tangle his fingers in that shimmering length of sunlit blond. He might pull her close, tilt back her head, look into her china-blue eyes and kiss her senseless.

He had to stop thinking these thoughts. His newly awakened awareness of Molly was inappropriate. And yet, he enjoyed these glimpses of her femininity more than he could say. Recognizing her charm was like finding buried treasure in your own backyard.

When she charged into the private room, he thought she was going to scoop her friend, Pierce, up in her arms and carry him out of here. Instead, she came to a sudden halt beside his bed, gracefully leaned down and placed a light kiss on his cheek. Holding his hand, she spoke gently, "You had me worried, old pal."

Pierce looked like hell. His pallor was emphasized by sunken cheeks and dark circles under his eyes. His cotton hospital gown hung limply from his broad shoulders. Managing a weak smile, he said, "They tell me I'm going to survive."

"When do you get out of here?"

"Maybe a week. Maybe sooner."

"Excellent." Pointedly, she counted the four huge bouquets that were placed around his hospital room. "Looks like you've got people who care about you."

"Florists," he said. "Business contacts. I pay their bills. You bet they care."

"They do care. We all care." Her lips pinched together. "I'm so sorry this happened to you."

"Me, too."

Adam's gut clenched. The two of them were talking as if Pierce had been injured in an accident instead of a deliberate assault. He reminded Molly, "We only have a few minutes."

Though she waved her hand to acknowledge his comment, she didn't take her eyes off Pierce. "Who attacked you? Do you have any idea?"

"Didn't see a thing," he said.

She nodded, accepting him at his word. "Is there anything I can do for you?"

"Don't investigate," he said.

That was a piece of good advice if Adam had ever heard one. Pierce rose several notches in his estimation.

"Why not?" she asked.

"Dangerous." His voice was already fading; he seemed at the end of his stamina. "I don't want you to get hurt."

The determined look on Molly's face told Adam that she wasn't about to listen to logic. She asked, "Do you think the attack on you was related to the magpie thefts?"

"I don't know."

"If it is," she said, "there's all the more reason for me to figure this out. You're not going to be safe until your thief is caught."

Inwardly, Adam groaned. She wasn't going to give up on this investigation.

"I'll figure this out," she said. "I'm not a quitter."

Pierce looked past Molly to Adam. "Make her back off."

"If I could," he said, "I would. But Molly is one stubborn lady. I've learned the hard way that I can't forbid her from doing anything."

Obviously exhausted, Pierce closed his eyelids. His voice was a whisper. "As long as you insist on being involved, there is something you could do for me."

"Tell me," Molly said.

"There's a wedding this weekend. Reception at the Brown Palace Hotel. The bride is Heidi…"

"I saw her," Molly said. "She's the bride who was having a fitting at Gloria's boutique."

"Right," he said. "If you can oversee the last details…"

"Perfect," she said. "I'm a great organizer. I'll keep your business on track until you're feeling better. Okay?"

Weakly, he nodded.

"I have your keys, and I'm sure I can find your appointment book in your office.

"Isn't my office a crime scene?"

"As if a piece of yellow tape is going to stop me? Don't you worry about a thing except getting better." Giving his hand a final squeeze, she stepped away from his bed. "Get well, pal."

"Thanks, Molly."

She stepped into the hallway and leaned against the wall, allowing the forced cheerfulness to fall from her face. Her blue eyes were rimmed with sadness, and Adam wished he could offer her an honest reassurance that they would find the thief and Pierce would be safe.

However, in his opinion, their chances of reaching a solution weren't good. The lack of forensic evidence, combined with Pierce's inability to identify his attacker, made investigation difficult. "Let's go, Molly. I need to pick up Amelia from the baby-sitter."

"I feel terrible about the attack on Pierce."

Were those tears in her eyes? His heart melted. It took all his self-control not to pull her into his arms, to hold her and to comfort her. "His injuries aren't your fault."

She swallowed hard. "But there should be more I can do."

The oppressive hospital atmosphere weighed down upon him, and he understood her frustration. He'd often felt the same way himself. It was like watching a car wreck in slow motion and being unable to stop the crash. "You feel powerless."

"Yes."

"The balance between right and wrong has been overturned, and it seems like there's nothing you can do to fix it."

"Totally."

There was a lot more Adam could say about the frustration that came from knowing disaster would strike. Being here in the hospital reminded him of his helplessness, his inability to stop the crash. But he kept his memories inside. He never discussed his private life or his personal feelings, not even with Molly. "Let's get out of here."

They went down the corridor, into the elevator, through the waiting area and into the outdoor pavilion where patients still hooked to IVs turned their faces to the sun. The crisp autumn weather embraced them, and Adam found himself breathing easier.

"Before we leave town," she said, "we ought to check in with Detective Berringer."

"I thought you hated him."

"I do," she said emphatically. "But Berringer was smart enough to ask for an inventory of Denny Devlin's knives. He might have uncovered some decent leads."

As a rule, Adam never used his position as the head of CCC to interfere in an ongoing police investigation. But he didn't think a simple phone call to Berringer would fall into that category. As they walked toward the parking lot, he placed the call on his cell phone, finally reaching Berringer.

After Adam identified himself, he asked, "Any new leads on the Pierce Williams stabbing?"

"What's your interest in this, Adam?"

Not wanting to admit that Molly had been pursuing an investigation that should have been the purview of the Denver PD, Adam stated the obvious. "Pierce is a friend of Molly's. She's concerned."

"She ought to be."

Adam frowned. Berringer's statement sounded vaguely like a threat. "Why do you think Molly should be concerned?"

"We have witnesses who saw someone going into Pierce's offices before the attack." Berringer paused. "The person they saw was Molly."

"Of course," Adam said. "She discovered the assault."

"Why didn't she place the 911 call?"

"I called 911," Adam said. "What are you getting at?"

"I'm not naming Molly as a suspect," the detective said in a tone that indicated otherwise. "But evidence shows she was the only person in Pierce's office. Her fingerprints are all over a lamp that was overturned. I need to talk to her again."

There was no mistaking his accusation. "You don't seriously believe she—"

"I've been checking the records, Adam. And it seems that several weddings where Pierce was the planner reported thefts."

"So?"

"Well, I know Molly's been on the straight and narrow since she's been working for you, but she has a record. Petty theft. Kiting checks."

"You're out of line, Berringer."

"Yeah? You want to tell me what Molly was doing at the crime scene?"

Adam had never lied to the police, and he wasn't about to start now by launching into a half-baked story about Molly's fake engagement to a kangaroo farmer. "I'll tell her that you're interested in another interview."

He disconnected the call and turned to Molly. "We have a problem."

MOLLY USED Pierce's keys to unlock the rear door to his shop and stalked inside. After Adam told her that Berringer considered her a suspect, she was outraged. In spite of all the good work she'd done at CCC, helping the police solve crimes, they suspected her. How could they? How dare they? She was a good person, a solid citizen, a taxpayer. "I'm not calling Berringer. No way. Not ever."

She stormed into Pierce's office and started yanking out the drawers on his desk, looking for his appointment book.

"Call him back," Adam said, "and tell him the truth."

"That I'm investigating crimes that the Denver PD should have taken more seriously? He'll be ticked off. He'll scold me for sticking my nose where it shouldn't be." In the middle drawer, she found Pierce's scheduling notebook. "Or maybe I should tell Berringer that I invented a fiancé and was pretending to be engaged. God, that sounds pathetic."

"The truth," Adam repeated. "You were trying to help out a friend."

As she slammed the drawer, frustration crashed around her. She glared across the office at Adam who leaned casually against the door frame. He was always calm and controlled, always respectful of authority. How could he possibly understand what it was like to be an outsider? To be unjustly accused?

She muttered, "I bet you're sorry that you agreed to be my partner."

"It doesn't work that way," he said.

"What do you mean?"

"When I offered to be your partner, that meant in good times and in bad. Just because we've hit a rough patch doesn't mean I'll desert you."

"This is one of those Marine Corps rules for living, isn't it? Like, never leave a man behind?"

A slow smile curved his mouth. "I'm an honorable man. Always have been. Always will be."

Consistency was Adam's life. And yet…he was different. She cocked her head, studying him curiously and enjoying her study. He'd never looked so appealing to her. There was something very masculine and sexy about the way he was honorably supporting her.

A strange warmth coiled through her—a sensual heat that had nothing to do with her anger at Berringer. "Does your sense of honor mean you'll stick with me while I continue to investigate?"

"I can't change your mind, so I guess I'm stuck." He pushed away from the wall. "Let's take a look at the crime scene."

As she left the office, she brushed against him, and the inadvertent physical contact fanned the flames that were growing inside her. It seemed impossible that she'd feel this way about Adam. For the past seven years, they'd been together constantly. They were friends. This ridiculous attraction had to stop!

As she entered the center area of Pierce's offices, a chill rose up inside her, throwing a bucket of ice water on her mood. Last night, she'd been terrified in this room. She remembered the shadows, the miasma of danger.

Unlike last night, there was enough daylight from the front window that this space wasn't completely in the dark. She easily found the light switch that had been invisible last night and turned on the overheads, illuminating the conference table and the wall of bridal photos. "Pierce's office space is separated into three parts. The plain back offices. The front reception area. And this room is where he and the brides do their actual planning."

As Adam confronted the display of bridal froufrou, he took a backward step, as though he'd been shoved in the chest. He stared at the photo display in shock.

"Are you scared?" she teased.

"Of course not."

But there was no mistaking his discomfort. His attitude amused her. This was a man who could pore over crime-scene photos, a man who liked a front row seat at autopsies. But show him a bit of lace and he became a quivering mass of raw nerve endings. "You don't like weddings, do you?"

"It's not my thing."

"Why? Because you don't like all the fuss? Because it's so girly?"

"Yeah. Maybe. I don't know." He was definitely flustered. "I don't like lingerie shops, either."

"But you like seeing women in lingerie."

"I appreciate the final result, but I don't much care

for knowing what went into it. Lace. Ruffles. Don't like it." He turned his back on the photo gallery. "Tell me what this room was like last night."

"Dark."

"I need details about exactly what happened. Walk me through it."

Though she hated to let him off the hook on his lingerie phobia, she nodded. She and Adam had done this kind of exercise before when they were trying to put together evidence. "Like I said, it was dark. I was looking for Pierce, calling his name. I barely glanced in this room. It's possible that someone was hiding here. Maybe behind the chairs."

"Concentrate, Molly. Did you hear anything? Did you sense movement?"

"I don't think so."

When she came around the partition into the front office, her gaze went immediately to the splotch of dried blood on the beige carpet. The stain was huge. My God, he'd lost so much blood. She swallowed hard and said, "Pierce was facedown. The knife handle stuck straight up in the center of his back."

She remembered the shock of seeing him—a jolt that knocked the air from her lungs. Initially, she hadn't been afraid. Her only thought was to help her friend.

"What about the lights?" Adam asked.

"Only the lamp on the desk was lit." She pointed. "And there was a glow from outside the windows, so the outdoor lights must have been on."

"And you tried the switch by the door," Adam said.

"It didn't work. Not until later, when all the lights burst on in a blinding flash."

"Okay," Adam said. "I think we can assume that the

person who attacked Pierce was playing with the breaker box."

"He was here," Molly said. "When I came in the back door, he must have still been here."

"Why didn't he leave?"

"The dead bolt on the front door was fastened, so he couldn't get out that way. He must have darkened the lights so I wouldn't see him."

"You were lucky," Adam said. "He could have come after you."

Her gaze returned to the obscene rust-colored stain on the carpet, and a shiver of apprehension went through her. Last night, she'd come closer than she thought to mortal danger.

"Another possibility," Adam said. "The attacker turned the lights off earlier so Pierce wouldn't know his identity."

"His or hers," Molly said, thinking of Gloria.

"That would mean the assailant was someone he knew."

"Of course, it was. That's the really awful thing about this. Somebody who knows Pierce is behind the magpie thefts and the backstabbing."

She recalled their three main suspects: Gloria, Denny Devlin and the photographer, Ronald Atchison. "Here's the part I don't understand. If the reason Pierce was stabbed was to cover up the magpie thefts, why didn't the attacker come after me? I'm the investigator."

"But you're undercover."

He circled the room, checking the position of the sofa and the coffee table. He reached down to rub away a trace of powder left behind by the forensic crew when they dusted for fingerprints.

"What are you looking for?"

"I want to know what happened here." He stepped cautiously around the bloodstain. "Describe the position of the body. Which way was Pierce lying?"

"His head was pointed toward the door."

"Which means the assailant came from the rear offices. He or she hit Pierce on the back of the head and he fell."

"That seems obvious," she said.

"Why was Pierce walking toward the door?"

"To lock up," she suggested.

"But the dead bolt was already fastened, and you found the keys in his pocket."

She squinted, trying to remember the scene. The lights in the office were out. The front dead bolt was locked. Why would Pierce be headed toward the door? "Maybe he was going across the street to get a cappuccino."

"But he was waiting for you to arrive."

"So he wouldn't have left," she said.

Adam hunkered down to study the carpet, and Molly did the same. From past experience with crime-scene photos, she knew they were looking for blood spatters that would indicate position and movement. Apart from her own bootprints, dragging blood smears across the floor, the stain was neatly contained in one place.

She drew a conclusion. "He didn't move after he was attacked."

"And I doubt he was in motion before the attack. There would have been a wider spatter."

"So he was just standing here. In the semidarkness."

"Right."

She ran her hand across the carpet fibers. "This is the first time I've analyzed an actual crime scene. Usually, when we do this kind of thing, we're in the office."

"Tell me what you think happened."

"Pierce was standing here. Not moving. I'd guess he was talking to someone who stood there." She pointed toward the door. "Someone else came up behind him and whacked him on the head. Then stabbed him."

Adam nodded. "There were two of them."

"That's the way it went down," she said with absolute certainty. Pierce had been engaged in a conversation, not expecting an attack. That explained why he didn't fight back. It made so much more sense than someone sneaking up on him. Pierce was an athletic guy with sharp reflexes. He would have fought back…unless he'd been taken completely off guard.

But whom had he been talking to? And why didn't he give the name to the police?

She stood slowly. Why didn't Pierce tell her about the conversation? "He didn't tell us everything. He lied to me, Adam."

"People do that."

But Pierce was her friend. They had a shared history. Maybe he didn't follow a strict code of honor like Adam, but Pierce was a decent guy. Loyal to the core. When everybody else abandoned Denny Devlin, Pierce stuck by him. "He must have had a good reason for lying to me."

"He could be protecting someone," Adam said.

"A person who tried to kill him? Who stabbed him in the back? He'd have to be crazy."

"Or caught in the grip of strong emotion. Like hate. Greed. Revenge. Or even love."

Gloria!

Chapter Seven

In spite of Adam's insistence that they needed to return to Golden immediately to pick up his niece from the baby-sitter, Molly couldn't pass up this opportunity to introduce him to Gloria before they left town. She went to the front door of Pierce's office and opened it. "While we're here, we've got to visit Gloria. Her shop is right next door."

"The bridal boutique?" He cringed. No doubt he was imagining himself being smothered in voile and ribbons. "No way. We don't have time to go there."

"But she's my number one suspect." Molly was struck with a particularly brilliant idea. "We should do the good cop/bad cop thing on Gloria. But I get to be the bad cop and maybe I should smack her around a bit."

"And blow your cover?"

"Just because I'm an undercover bride, it doesn't mean I'm a sissy."

"Hell, no," he muttered. "Tell me why you suddenly zoomed in on Gloria as your number one suspect."

"If Pierce lied to me to protect someone, it's got to be her. Poor, misguided Pierce once loved that nasty woman enough to marry her."

"But he divorced her," Adam said.

"Which doesn't mean he stopped loving her." She shuddered at the thought of her friend Pierce in the manicured clutches of Gloria the Grotesque. "Or maybe it's not love, but business."

"Explain."

"Who knows what happened in the divorce? She might have some kind of leverage over him. Maybe he's protecting her so she won't destroy his business."

"We'll see her," Adam said. "Five minutes at the bridal boutique. If we're going to be on time to pick up Amelia, I should allow for rush hour traffic."

"Not a problem." As they exited onto the street, Molly pulled out her cell phone to call the baby-sitter, a sweet-faced single mom with a daughter who was the same age as Amelia. "I'll tell the sitter we might be a little late."

It was only a few paces along the sidewalk to the bridal boutique. Still on the phone, Molly pushed open the door and swept inside with Adam following close behind. Gloria—dressed in a sleek, oatmeal-colored jersey dress that emphasized her greyhound body—stood beside the window display talking to a short man with a gray goatee. She didn't look happy to see them.

While Adam introduced himself, Molly completed her phone call. The sitter was okay with them being late.

Clicking the cell phone closed, Molly faced Pierce's ex-wife. "Sorry," she said. "I was talking to our baby-sitter."

Gloria raised an eyebrow as she glanced first at Adam, then at Molly. "You two have a child?"

"Us?" This was worse than having people assume Adam was her fiancé. "A child? No."

"My niece," Adam explained. "I work with Molly. You might even say we're partners."

"How entertaining for you, Adam." Gloria's lips thinned in a sneering smile, then her gaze focused on Molly again. "I see you have Pierce's appointment book."

"I visited him at the hospital, and he asked me to take care of the details for Heidi's wedding this weekend."

"Don't be absurd," Gloria said. "You know nothing about wedding protocol. Give me the book."

Molly yanked it away from her. "I'm handling this. It's the least I can do for Pierce. He almost died."

"I know." Gloria looked down. Was she struck by a grief? Or covering her lack of emotion? "I spoke to the hospital. He's expected to recover."

"But he won't be able to work the wedding this weekend," Molly said. "And I'll take care of his business in the meantime."

The man with the goatee stepped forward. "You're in charge?"

"Yes," Molly said. "And you are?"

"I am Lucien Smythe." He stuck out his chest and lifted his chin. He was the very picture of dignity and pride. "I am the proprietor and owner of Lucien Smythe Jewelry."

Since Molly assumed his connection to the wedding biz was engagement rings and wedding bands, she made sure he could see the flash of her diamonds. "Pleased to meet you."

"A lovely ring," he said. "May I take a closer look?"

Molly placed her hand in his. Though he wasn't a tall man, his fingers were long and elegant. They were artistic hands, and his touch was smooth as ivory. When he finished his appraisal of the engagement ring that had belonged to Adam's mother, he gazed up at her and smiled kindly. "These are good diamonds of fine clarity."

"They are?" Gloria sounded surprised.

"That's right," Molly snapped. "I didn't get my engagement ring from a Cracker Jack box."

"Very fine," Lucien said.

"My fiancé," Molly said, "has excellent taste."

"The value of this ring is more than the stones," the jeweler said. "The style is forty-five to fifty years old. May I venture a guess?"

"Yes," she said.

"I see the love in your eyes," he said.

"You do?"

"And your fiancé must love you very much. This ring belonged to his mother. Therefore, it is priceless."

His sincerity touched her. She instinctively liked this artistic little man, and she felt creepy about lying to him, pretending to be engaged. "Thank you, Lucien."

"Now we must speak of business," he said. "I had arranged with Pierce to loan some of my antique jewelry for the wedding this weekend. After the attack on him last night, I am concerned about security."

"Which is why he came to me," Gloria said. "I assured him there was no problem with the loan of the jewels."

Adam stepped forward. "How much is this jewelry worth?"

"Approximately eight hundred thousand dollars," Lucien said.

"What are your usual security measures?"

"I personally accompany all loaned jewelry. I attend the ceremony and the reception." He pulled aside the lapel of his jacket, revealing a shoulder holster. "And I am always armed."

Molly had no doubt that this small, neat man with the elegant hands wouldn't hesitate to shoot a thief.

"Would you be more comfortable if I arranged for two or three more armed security guards?"

"It's a wedding," Gloria snapped. "We can't have policemen in uniforms—"

"They'll be in tuxedos," Molly said. Through CCC, she was in contact with several volunteers, mostly retired military, who enjoyed doing security work and were very good at it. "Don't worry. These gentlemen are former officers in the military. One of them was a Navy SEAL."

"Like Jesse Ventura," Gloria said coldly. "That's not acceptable. May I remind you that this reception is at the Brown Palace Hotel. Very posh. Very A-list. We can't have thugs bumbling around."

Adam took a step forward. "Did you say thugs?"

Lucien stood beside him. He glared at Gloria. "I was in the Navy."

"My dear gentlemen, you misunderstand." Gloria backed down gracefully. "I never meant to imply any negative criticism of our brave military personnel."

When Lucien reached into his inner jacket pocket, Molly hoped he was pulling his pistol to shoot Gloria in the foot.

No such luck. He opened an engraved gold case and took out his business card which he handed to Molly. "I would be delighted to have your thugs as security guards for my jewelry. Please arrange for them to meet me at my shop before the wedding."

He turned on his heel and left the boutique.

As soon as he was gone, Gloria pounced. "Why are you here, Molly? Did you want to try on another gown?"

Molly really wanted to play the "bad cop." She really wished she could ask the hard questions that would make Gloria squirm. But she wasn't sure of what those questions were.

She glanced over at Adam who was eyeballing the wedding gowns suspiciously. If one of these dresses made a false move, he would undoubtedly hack it to death with his black belt in karate moves.

"My own wedding plans," Molly said, "will be put on hold until Pierce is well. I came here to give you an update on his condition."

"I spoke to the hospital," she said.

"But I spoke directly to him. Face-to-face."

Though Molly watched Gloria carefully for a guilty reaction, Pierce's ex-wife was utterly stoic. Not a single hair in her sleek black bob moved. "What did he say?"

"He was very weak."

"And?" Gloria lifted her chin. "Does he have any idea who did this terrible thing?"

"He didn't see his attacker," Molly said. "At least, he doesn't remember seeing his attacker. That's a common reaction. People who have been in a traumatic event sometimes don't remember what happened. Then, all of a sudden, their memory comes back."

"That doesn't sound medical," Gloria said.

"It's true. I've had experience with this before." Molly glared accusingly at Gloria. "And when Pierce remembers, he can name names. Right, Adam?"

"Yes." He nodded stiffly. "Common reaction."

Though Molly doubted that Gloria would burst out with a confession, she said, "Tell me about last night. What happened?"

"I haven't the slightest idea," she said. "I was here, working late with Stan."

"Stan?" Adam asked.

"Stan Lansky," she repeated. "He's my tailor. We're terribly busy with the final preparations for the wedding this weekend. There are five bridesmaids and one of these dear little things is pregnant, requiring nearly impossible alterations in her gown."

"Last night," Molly said. "Did you hear anything from Pierce's office next door?"

"Not a sound," Gloria said. "This is one of the older buildings in Cherry Creek North. Solid brick with thick walls."

Molly glanced toward the rear of the shop where the inventory was kept and the tailor had his workspace. "What about Stan? Did he hear anything?"

"If he did, I'm sure he would have mentioned it to the police."

Gloria rested her hands on her hips. In her snug jersey outfit, she was so skinny that she looked like a stick figure Amelia might have drawn to hang on Adam's refrigerator. But there was nothing childlike or innocent about Gloria. She was pure, sophisticated evil.

Molly blurted. "It's hard to believe you and Pierce were a couple. You're so different."

"Maybe not as much as you think," she said.

"But you are," Molly insisted. "Pierce is open and athletic and friendly. You seem…the opposite."

"That's a very simplified analysis," Gloria said. "You know nothing about me. Nothing about my past. Nothing about my triumphs and my failures."

"Tell me."

"I think not," Gloria said. "All that you need to know about me is that I have impeccable taste and I'm very good at my work."

"How did you and Pierce start working together?"

"Quite naturally. When it comes to wedding plans,

we're a good match. He brings a certain vitality. And I give him a much needed dose of class."

When she explained it that way, Molly could almost understand their relationship. They were complementary, like the yin and yang of wedding planners. "And in your marriage?"

"None of your business." Though her words were clipped, Gloria's dark eyes flickered with something akin to real emotion. "I don't wear my heart on my sleeve. You will never see me burst into tears. You will never hear me sob. But make no mistake, I am concerned about Pierce. Deeply concerned. The attack on him...devastated me."

Then, Gloria straightened her shoulders. "Is there anything else I can help you with this afternoon?"

"Not right now. But I'll be in touch."

Molly frowned as she exited Gloria's Bridal Boutique with Adam at her side. Though she wanted to see Gloria as the person responsible for the attack on Pierce, she wasn't so sure. *He gave her vitality. She gave him class.* They actually were a much better match than Molly had assumed.

Inside Pierce's office, she turned to Adam. "Apart from your outright hostility toward the wedding gowns, what did you think? Did she do it?"

He went to the solid wall that separated Pierce's office from that of his ex-wife and wrapped his knuckles against it. "Solid."

"What are you doing?"

"According to the police, no one was seen entering or leaving this office. Except for you."

That didn't surprise Molly. The rear entrance to the shop was fairly well concealed from traffic on the street. "So?"

"There might be a communicating door between the two shops."

"Like a secret passage?" She was all over that idea. "That would be so cool."

"While we're here, we might as well check it out."

She walked along beside him as he inspected the walls and moldings. "I'm not very good at being objective. At first, my gut reaction was that Gloria was responsible for the attack on Pierce. Mostly because I don't like her."

"She's not likable."

"But I think I've changed my mind. When she was talking about how devastated she was, I wanted to offer a shoulder for her to cry on."

"You're softhearted," Adam said.

"I guess that's not a very useful trait for a detective."

"The worst," he said. "When you're investigating, you need to suspect everyone. You need to look on the dark side."

"How can I do that?"

"Turn off your emotions," he said. "Think like an investigator. Look for evidence. We've talked about this before. You know the three basic things to look for."

"Method. Motive. And opportunity," she recited. So many times in the office, they'd gone over those three basic elements in the search for evidence. "Let's start with method."

"We have the weapon," Adam said. "A special gourmet knife. Would Gloria have access to such a weapon?"

"She might." Gloria was such a snob that she probably had the very best in cooking tools. "There's a kitchenette in the rear of her boutique, but I doubt she'd have a carving knife lying around."

"Also, regarding method, I believe our analysis of a two-person attack is plausible."

Molly nodded. "At least one of those people is someone Pierce knows well enough to be having a conversation in his office after closing time."

Adam moved into the center room to check the walls. "So, we'll talk about opportunity. Gloria's alibi is this Stan person, the tailor."

"But she was right next door," Molly said. "She could have sneaked over here without Stan missing her and attacked Pierce."

"You saw her when the paramedics arrived," Adam said. "If she stabbed Pierce, she would have been covered in blood."

She conjured up a clear memory of last night. There had been blood, but the smears were all on Molly. Her sleeves. Her boots. "Gloria was clean."

"What about the tailor?"

"Stan?" She couldn't imagine that rabbity little man stabbing anybody, much less Pierce, who was nearly a foot taller than he was. "I don't think so. And he didn't have blood on him."

"What about Denny Devlin? He claimed to be at his shop, but what if he'd come here for the meeting with you?"

She had to agree with his conclusion. "And we really don't know anything about the whereabouts of Ronald, our third suspect."

"Which brings us to motive," Adam said. "If your theory about the magpie thief being involved in the stabbing is true, I doubt Gloria did it. She doesn't impress me as the sort of woman who would steal gravy boats and toasters."

"Then there must be a different motive." Molly

didn't want to give up on Gloria as a suspect. "She and Pierce were involved in all sorts of business dealings."

She trailed behind Adam as he moved into the third area—the plain rear offices. He peered behind the file cabinets. As he leaned down, she was distracted by the rear view. His broad shoulders tapered nicely to a firm torso. He had an excellent butt—probably from clenching all the time.

She sank into the chair behind Pierce's desk and refocused her thoughts on the crime. "If it was Gloria, why did she choose last night to attack?"

Adam completed his inspection of the walls without finding a secret passageway. He turned to her and said, "We have new information to add to our investigation."

"What's that?"

"Diamonds. Eight hundred thousand dollars worth of antique jewelry from Lucien Smythe."

"What about it?"

"The loaned jewelry is a worthy target for a thief. Possibly, the other robberies were a setup for a bigger haul."

"Not likely," she said. "Practice at stealing isn't really how it works. For a big heist, a thief doesn't want to attract attention. If the mark is aware, security gets amped up."

"The mark?"

"The target of the theft," she explained.

"I know what a mark is," he said. "I don't like to hear you use that slang."

She met his gaze. Though Adam knew all about her nefarious past, he'd never been comfortable with the knowledge that she was capable of picking his pocket at any given moment. He'd rather pretend that she didn't have a life before she came to work for him. "I know about these things, Adam. Somebody who gets excited by petty theft, like these wedding robberies, isn't a mastermind who would go after eight hundred thou in antique jewels. Our magpie is just that. A magpie. Attracted to shiny objects."

"Why?"

"There are lots of possible reasons. Petty revenge. To get attention. Or for the thrill."

"The thrill?"

"You're getting away with something. Your heart beats a little faster. You feel more alive."

Usually, this would be the end of the conversation. Adam would turn and walk away from her, shaking his head and mumbling. Instead, he continued to gaze into her eyes. "Did stealing give you a thrill, Molly?"

Defiantly, she lifted her chin. "I'm not going to apologize for what I used to do. Because it's over. Totally in the past. Working for CCC all these years, I've seen the other side. The victim's side. I can empathize with what it's like to be robbed. Violated. I know right from wrong."

"I know you do."

His gaze took on a gentle, distracted glow. She recognized the expression because she'd seen it before on dozens of other men. But not Adam. Never on Adam. *He was looking at her as though he wanted to kiss her.*

No way! She had to be mistaken.

When she rose from the desk chair, she was standing close to Adam. They were only a few feet apart. What would happen if she kissed him? Damn, she knew better. She and Adam had a good working relationship—a great working relationship. They were friends. Nothing destroyed a friendship with a man quicker than sex. Intimacy made everything weird.

"We should go," she said. "It's time to pick up Amelia."

"Right."

He stepped back to let her pass, and she eased self-consciously past him.

After she'd locked up Pierce's offices, she glanced toward Adam again. He was back to his regular demeanor, checking his wristwatch and scowling at the passage of time. "Hurry it up, Molly."

"The sitter said we could be late."

"You know how I feel about punctuality."

"It's your mantra," she said. He was always *where* he was supposed to be *when* he was supposed to be there. As she glanced toward him, every hint of sexuality was gone.

She must have imagined that glow. Adam would never change.

Chapter Eight

The computer screen at Molly's desk in the Colorado Crime Consultants offices blinked rapidly in response to her typed queries. She was comfortable here in her lumbar-support desk chair with her favorite knick-knacks on her desk. No family photos, of course. Though she had dozens of foster care parents, there were none she remembered with particular fondness. And her real parents? The last time she heard from her father, he was in prison in California. She had no idea where her drug-addicted mother might be. Rehab? Jail? The closest Molly could come to a family photo was an array of mug shots.

The past didn't matter. She'd turned out okay.

A thought crossed her mind, and her fingers danced across the keyboard. This desk was her battle station during a CCC investigation. Usually, though, she had more focus from investigators in the field. In a typical case that fell under CCC scrutiny, new evidence had been uncovered. They had tangible suspicions to follow up on.

In spite of the fact that Molly herself had discovered Pierce after the attack, she didn't have a clear idea about motive. Why had the magpie stolen various objects from weddings? How did those meaningless thefts lead to the attack on Pierce?

Accessing the database for the FBI's National Crime Information Center, Molly found no criminal record for Gloria Vanderly or her tailor, Stan Lansky. There was a DUI for the caterer, Dennis Devlin. Ronald Atchison, the wedding photographer, had a couple of white collar criminal charges and one conviction for fraud.

She typed in Lucien Smythe's name and waited while the NCIC information bank whipped through a massive number of crimes, criminals and missing persons. The sheer volume of wrongdoing was depressing. Adam sometimes said that half the population was running around committing crimes while the other half tried to catch them. Kind of a cynical attitude, but that was Adam. His world view was black and white, good and bad, right and wrong.

The system paused; she had a hit. Lucien Smythe, the jeweler, had been charged, six years ago, with assault. Molly flipped through several other information sources until she had the whole story. Someone had tried to rob Lucien's jewelry store. There was a fight. Lucien won.

Molly frowned at the screen. The jeweler had been defending himself and his merchandise. Why would he be charged? She read further. Before calling the police, Lucien had sliced off the thief's pinky finger. Ew! Molly cringed. Though she could understand Lucien's outrage, violent mutilation went beyond the acceptable limits of self-defense.

Nonetheless, the charges against Lucien were dropped. He was reinstated as a solid citizen with a permit to carry a gun.

This detail from his past was worth noting. Lucien

had used a knife on the thief, and she had to wonder if it was a high-carbon, stainless steel chef's knife from Germany.

Her gaze drifted to the window. Outside the office, dusk had settled. It was after six o'clock, and she'd promised to meet Adam and Amelia for dinner at seven. One more phone call, and she'd head over to his house.

For the fourth time, she punched in the phone number for Ronald Atchison. Though expecting to hear his answering machine again, Ronald himself picked up.

She identified herself and said, "I'm so glad I finally caught you. We need to set up a meeting. Tomorrow?"

"Sweetie, I can't wait to see you." His voice was smooth and warm as scented oil. Ronald was a sensual man—classically tall, dark and handsome. "You're my type of woman, Miss Molly. Tall and vivacious with masses of blond hair and cleavage like the prow of the *Queen Mary.*"

She grinned at the phone. "Thanks, I think."

"The last time I saw you was at a party."

She remembered. "At Pierce's downtown loft."

"And you were wearing burgundy sequins."

"Right," Molly said. "And you wondered if my dress came in your size."

"Indeed, I did." Ronald regularly put his gorgeousness on display as a different kind of queen—a drag queen. "I can't believe you're getting married and need a photographer. I hope my humble services will suffice."

"Humble?" That had never been Ronald's style.

"I'm so fabulous that I've gone full circle back to self-deprecating," he said. "Rather charming, if I do say so myself."

Charming and clever. Though it was hard for her to

imagine Ronald as an assassin, Molly thought the photographer might be tempted by the magpie thefts. He might get a thrill out of stealing small objects and stirring up trouble.

She asked, "Have you heard about Pierce?"

"Dreadful."

"Who do you think did it?"

"It's all about the money, honey."

"How so?"

"Are you sure you want to hear my theory?" he asked. "You know how much I love to lecture."

"Do tell, Ronald."

"Wedding economics are largely based on what the market can bear. The fixed cost of my film is the same whether I'm taking photos in the park or doing a formal sitting. If Pierce tells the blushing bride that I'm the very best, I can charge more." He paused. "Obviously, that wouldn't apply to you."

"Money is no problem," she said. "My fiancé is loaded."

"Good golly, Miss Molly. I'd expect no less from a babe such as yourself."

Though she enjoyed Ronald's banter and didn't want to believe he was a suspect, she simply had to stop seeing the good side of people. If she meant to be a real detective, she needed to be more distrustful. "Tell me more about wedding economics. Why would the money cause somebody to attack Pierce?"

"Weddings are expensive. Insanely expensive. Even a penny-pinching bride on a budget reaches a point when she's throwing money around like a drunken sailor, telling herself that it's *her* day. She deserves it."

"What does that have to do with Pierce?"

"The wedding planner is influential in where the

money gets spent. And how it gets spent. Cheap daisies or imported orchids? Faux fur or mink? Maybe Pierce withheld a lucrative contract."

Though it was difficult for her to imagine a knife-wielding florist or a homicidal wedding cake baker, there was merit to Ronald's opinion. "You might be right."

"There's a dark side to all this gauze and glitz," Ronald said ominously. "Pierce makes a lot of money planning weddings. You really ought to look into his business dealings."

"Save me the time," she said. "Did Pierce ever cause you to lose a contract?"

"I don't recall."

She didn't believe him. Though Ronald acted the role of a flamboyant artist, he was a businessman at heart—a businessman who had been convicted of fraud.

After Molly explained that she was taking over Pierce's business while he was in the hospital, she set an appointment with Ronald for the following day. "We also need to talk about Heidi's wedding at the Brown Palace this weekend."

"The petite bride," he said with a groan. "I'll need to be careful in the ceremony photos so she won't look like a munchkin."

It occurred to Molly that Ronald had taken photos at all the weddings where thefts had occurred. Seeing those pictures might be useful. "Do you keep copies of your photos?"

"I hold the negatives for a couple of years," he said. "Sometimes a bride will want to reorder."

She scanned her research information and found the name for the wedding where jewelry was stolen at the reception. "How about at the Deitrich wedding? Did you take candids at the reception?"

"Do you still work for that investigation place?"

"Colorado Crime Consultants," she said.

"Are you playing detective, Miss Molly?"

"Of course not." There was too much bluster in her voice. After seven years with Adam, her lying skills were sadly out of practice. "I'm engaged. I've got a ring. I just want to see what kind of candids you do."

"Not convinced," Ronald said. "If I were you, sweetheart, I wouldn't get involved."

"Why not?"

"See you tomorrow," he said. "Wear something fantastic."

"I always do."

She disconnected the call. Why had he told her not to get involved? She had to wonder if he meant to threaten her or to warn her. Either way, it was obvious that Ronald knew more than he was saying.

On the other hand, his advice seemed solid. *It's all about the money, honey.* She needed to delve more deeply into Pierce's business dealings. Tomorrow morning, that's where she'd start.

Tonight, she had dinner with Adam and Amelia.

After locking up, she left the CCC headquarters and followed the sidewalk to the rear parking area. It was a lovely evening for October. Clear and clean. In the early night sky, the stars were already out. It seemed much later than seven. No one else was on the street. Shadowy foothills loomed closely around her.

As she approached the parking lot, a shiver went through her. She had the sense that someone was watching her—and not in a good way. These eyes from the dark weren't the gaze of an admirer. Molly glanced over her shoulder. She saw no one.

Hustling across the parking lot, the high heels of her

boots hit the asphalt with hard clicks. Was she imagining danger? Or did she have a real cause for alarm? It was smart to assume the latter. She remembered the terror she'd felt in Pierce's office when she was taken by surprise and was too terrified to react. That wouldn't happen again. If anyone came at her, she'd be ready for him. She held her car keys with the sharp edge protruding through her knuckles. A hard blow from her fist would be painful.

Her lavender Volkswagen was parked with the nose facing a narrow row of conifers that separated the small asphalt lot from a darkened house up the hill. Parked a couple of spaces down was a white van—the type of anonymous vehicle used for deliveries. She didn't see a logo on the side.

She pointed her car keys and clicked, hearing the reassuring chirp of the car doors unlocking. Her hand was on the door handle when the side door of the van swept open.

A tall figure dressed all in black leapt out. The face was a blank—hidden behind a black ski mask. In the gloved hand of the attacker, Molly saw the gleam of a blade.

With no time to think, she reacted. Braced against the side of her car, she lashed out with a fierce kick, aimed at the knees of her attacker. The tall figure darted back.

Molly swung with her purse.

The worst mistake she could make was to allow her assailant to get close enough to do damage with the knife.

Self-defense lessons from Adam told her to aim for the knees, the groin and the throat. And to make noise.

With a loud yell, Molly kicked again. Her legs were long, and her boot heels were lethal weapons. Her assailant backed off.

Beside her, the interior of the van gaped like the maw of a beast. No way in hell would Molly get herself thrown in there. She had to act fast.

With another yell, she yanked open the door to her car. The interior light flashed on. If she could get inside the Volks, she'd be safe.

But she couldn't turn her back on her attacker.

A weapon! She needed a weapon.

Groping around inside her car, Molly found the long plastic brush she used to wipe winter snow off her car. Using the long brush like a sword, she charged at the attacker who backed off a few more paces.

Taking advantage of her attack position, Molly kicked high and fast. Her boot heel connected with the attacker's thigh. Another kick. The assailant tumbled backward, off balance and fell.

Now! Molly raced to her car. Safely in the driver's seat, she slammed and locked the door. She'd won! She'd escaped without a scratch. Plugging the key into the ignition, she cranked the engine and whipped into reverse.

Her attacker had disappeared into the van. The sliding door closed.

Molly's heart hammered inside her rib cage. Her fingers clamped around the steering wheel, and her foot hit the accelerator. Speeding like white lightning, she drove two blocks toward the central business area.

She'd done it! She'd escaped! She'd thought fast and moved even faster. Like a kung fu princess. Bring on the crouching tigers and hidden dragons. She could handle them!

It was only after she'd driven a few blocks that she realized she'd made a mistake. A big one.

She should have stayed with the van, followed it,

taken the license number. She should have called the police so they could apprehend the villain.

Too late now. Her attacker was gone—vanished into the night in a bland white van. She had nothing to show for the assault but a wildly elevated heart rate and the suddenly terrifying sense that someone had tried to kill her.

SOMEWHERE IN THE BACK of his mind, Adam had known that he shouldn't leave her at the office unprotected. He'd made a mistake, and his carelessness had almost cost Molly her life.

Arms folded, he leaned against the granite countertop in his kitchen. Tension spread through his muscles. He could feel the vein in his forehead begin to throb. It wasn't like him to be so lax during the course of an investigation. He'd been lulled into complacency. All those bridal veils and fancy gowns had masked the cutthroat nature of the wedding business.

For the second time in as many days, he listened as Molly told him about a near escape from danger.

"I was really cool," she said. "I remembered everything you've ever told me about aiming for the knees and the groin and making a lot of noise. And then I grabbed my snow cleaning thingy and used it like a sword."

"The plastic snow scraper?"

"That's right." She went into an *en garde* stance. "Maybe I should take up fencing."

Adam glanced through the kitchen door toward Amelia who was playing quietly in the living room. Though he didn't want to bring his niece into this discussion, there wasn't a choice. They needed to contact the police and make a full report. Then, he needed to arrange for a bodyguard for Molly.

As she stalked back and forth across the terra-cotta tile in his kitchen, he could tell that her adrenaline level was still high. The first time she'd been threatened in Pierce's office, she exhibited all the classic signs of fear. This time, she appeared to be excited. Her cheeks flushed red. Her blue eyes glistened.

His natural inclination was to give her hell, to tell her that she shouldn't take risks, to scare her into being cautious. At the same time, he didn't want to undermine her confidence. Keeping his voice level, he said, "You did well, Molly."

"Damn right." Her ferocious grin seemed shaky at the edges. "I was totally kick-ass."

"Did you get a license plate number?"

She lashed out with a couple of high kicks. "I hit him once. In the thigh."

"Him?"

"Hah!" She kicked again, balancing easily on her high-heeled boots. "That's one bad guy who's going to be limping."

"You're sure it was a man."

"No." With both feet on the floor, she exhaled a gush of air. "This person was tall, dressed in a bulky parka and a ski mask. And the light in the parking lot was dim. It could have been a woman."

"Gloria?"

"I don't know." Another sigh. The bravado was draining from her. "Everything happened so fast. At the same time, it was like slo-mo with each second passing in a tick. Why is that?"

"Level of intensity," he said. "A fight that seems to last for hours only takes a few seconds in real time. It's like making love."

Her eyebrows lifted. "How so?"

Adam regretted the comparison. He hadn't wanted to go in this direction; his newly awakened awareness of Molly was an unsafe topic. Time to change the subject. "We should call the police."

"Wait a minute," she said. "You mentioned something about levels of intensity and making love."

"Yes, I did."

"And?"

He knew from years of working with her that she wouldn't let go of this topic until he explained. Aware that he was venturing into dangerous waters, he kept his voice level and calm. "When you make love, your senses are heightened." He couldn't believe he was saying this. Who the hell did he think he was? Dr. Phil? "Your brain is forced to interpret an excess of sensual information. Therefore, it seems like time slows down."

She nodded. "The more intense the experience, the longer it seems to take."

"Right," he said. "Now we should call the police."

"Sometimes a kiss that only lasts for a minute goes on forever," she said. "And it changes your whole life."

He picked up the mobile phone and held it toward her. "911, Molly."

She pushed the phone back at him. "I can't identify the van except to say that it was white. I didn't think to get a license plate number. All I can tell the police about my attacker is that he or she was tall and had a knife."

"Not much to go on," Adam agreed. "All the same, we need to follow procedure."

"I never thought I'd be so bad as a witness."

"Not your fault," he said.

"But I know better. I'm a detective."

"It's okay, Molly. The important thing is that you're safe."

He flung an arm around her shoulder, intending to offer friendly comfort. But her nearness had a more profound effect on his senses. The natural scent of her body mingled enticingly with the kitchen aromas. She radiated heat, sensual heat.

Leaning against his chest, she trembled slightly, and his awareness of her body increased. Though she was lean and not soft, her curves were gently feminine. Her hips flared from an hourglass waist. The side of her breast rubbed against his chest.

"Adam," she said softly. "I don't want to call the cops. Please."

"They need to investigate."

"I can't stand to see Berringer smirking, telling me how dumb I was. He'll probably turn this around to be my fault. I should have tailed the van and called 911 on my cell phone."

"You followed your instincts." He fought to ignore the tendrils of her gleaming blond hair that tickled his cheek. He was finding it difficult to be calm and controlled. It was damn ironic that he'd just been lecturing her about sensual overload. "You had to escape. That was the number one concern. And now, we call the police."

"I know we should. It's the right thing to do." She tilted her head to look up at him. "But there's nothing the police can do."

There was a dangerous logic in what she said. Normally, he would never hesitate in following correct procedure.

"Please don't call them," she said.

His resolve faded. At that moment, he was so damned grateful that she hadn't been hurt that he couldn't refuse her request. He'd break any rule to make her happy. All he wished for was to continue holding her and to see her smile.

He cleared his throat. "Just this once, we can deviate from protocol."

"Thanks." She beamed.

"But we can't pretend this attack didn't happen," he said. "You can't go home alone tonight. You're staying here where I can keep an eye on you."

He braced himself for an argument that didn't come. Instead, she nodded. "I'm glad you offered."

"You are?"

"I know when I need protecting. And that time is right now."

As she stepped out of his arms and went toward the living room where Amelia was playing, his gaze feasted on her sexy gait. She was incredible. And she was spending the night.

Inwardly, he groaned. It was going to be hell to sleep under the same roof but not in the same bed. Damn it, he ought to be more careful about what he wished for.

Chapter Nine

In spite of the fact that she'd been menaced by a knife-wielding psycho, this wasn't the worst day of Molly's life. Not by a long shot. There was her marriage. And her divorce. Her bankruptcy. The car repo. Being hired at a pathetic minimum-wage job. Being fired from the same job. Most of her life had been a precarious day-by-day battle.

Then Adam came along. He'd given her a chance, and that changed everything. He was more than her boss, more than her mentor. She could always look to Adam for stability. If she hadn't been able to come here tonight, Molly didn't know what she would have done.

They had just tucked Amelia into bed after a story of Cinderella the poodle with two rottweilers as the ugly stepsisters. Later tonight, Molly would slip into this guest room queen-size bed to sleep beside little Amelia.

For now, she returned to Adam's masculine living room and sat in a heavy beige suede chair with her feet propped on an ottoman. Earlier, she'd showered and changed from her red leather pantsuit into one of his long flannel plaid shirts and white athletic socks. She wasn't much to look at after washing her hair and letting it dry straight, but she was totally relaxed, hanging out with an old and trusted pal.

He came from the kitchen carrying two snifters. Without a word, he placed one in her hand. Then he settled into an overstuffed chair opposite her and swirled the golden liquid in the bulbous glass.

"This is a first," she said.

"A first what?"

"Ever since I started working for you, we've had a routine. Every evening at exactly six o'clock, you come out of your office, and I hand you a glass with three fingers of Jack Daniel's." She gazed down into the snifter. "This is the first time you've ever served me a drink. Cognac?"

"Courvoisier," he said.

"I thought the one glass of Jack was the only alcohol you allowed yourself."

"You really don't know very much about me, Molly."

It wasn't for lack of prying. When they first met, she made a concentrated effort to learn something of his history. All she'd uncovered were the basics: He was briefly married once and divorced. No children. He had one sister. His father was in the Marine Corps, and his family lived all over the place. Adam had a distinguished military career of his own and was awarded two Purple Hearts.

He wasn't the type of guy who confided details about his past. Consistently, he brushed aside her questions, saying she was on a "need-to-know" basis.

"Here's to you, Adam Briggs." She held up her snifter in a toast. "Now I know that you indulge in the occasional nightcap. And you buy the good stuff."

She took a sip and savored the rich liqueur. Even to her untrained palate, the flavor was remarkable—

creamy, with a tongue-tingling bite. There seemed to be a faint citrus aroma, like orange blossoms in the spring. Definitely, this was the good stuff.

"Now that Amelia has gone to bed," he said, "we need to talk about what happened to you in the parking lot."

He got right down to business. That was so typically Adam. "Right."

"Describe your attacker."

"Tall, but not freakish like a basketball player or anything." She closed her eyes to concentrate, trying to relive those terrifying moments when a shadow leapt from the van. "It's kind of a blur."

"Give me your impressions."

She shook her head, frustrated. "The person was dressed all in black. Black ski mask. Black parka. I saw the flash of a knife blade. It could have been Gloria or Denny Devlin or even Ronald Atchison."

"Who?"

"Ronald is a photographer. We're going to meet with him tomorrow. He's the third name on my list of magpie suspects."

She opened her eyes and indulged in another sip of Courvoisier. "But it couldn't be Ronald because I talked to him only minutes before I went outside."

"The height," Adam said, "eliminates some people."

She nodded. "It wasn't Lucien Smythe. Or the tailor at Gloria's shop."

"What about the vehicle?"

"A generic white van. The kind that's used for deliveries. There wasn't a logo on the side, but it might have been covered up. I'll bet most of the wedding people use delivery vans. For sure, Denny Devlin, the caterer, would."

Adam made a grumbling noise deep in his throat, and she gazed over the rim of her snifter at him. It wasn't an unpleasant view. His features were perfectly balanced. His firm stubborn jaw matched his broad forehead etched with fine worry lines. His deep-set blue eyes regarded her steadily, almost curiously. As if he didn't know her face? They'd been together almost every day for seven years. They knew each other's habits better than some married couples.

"What are you thinking?" she asked.

"The obvious question—why were you attacked?"

"Beats me."

"You must have stumbled across some kind of clue."

Unfortunately, she had no idea what significant detail she might have uncovered. "I don't know what."

"Tell me everything you've uncovered so far."

She rattled through all the data from her search of the NCIC crime database, including the interesting story about Lucien Smythe and the burglar.

"He cut off the guy's pinky," Adam said. "That's a little scary."

"And he looks like such a mild-mannered fellow."

"What else?"

She remembered Ronald Atchison's advice about looking into the big bucks generated by weddings. "I started going through financials for Pierce's business. His profit and loss statements. Lines of credit. The loan to Denny Devlin, which is, by the way, truly substantial. There are a couple of red flags I should check out."

"Unusual withdrawals of cash?"

"Not really. Pierce makes a lot more money than I thought. He's mentioned real estate investments, but I really need to see his personal records to have a complete picture."

"How could you access those records?"

"I assume they're at his town house. We could go there tomorrow."

"Sounds like a starting place."

Adam rose from his chair and paced toward the fireplace that was the main feature in this cozy room. Resting his elbow on the mantel, he looked every inch the lord of the manor. Innately, he had the bearing of a leader.

"I wonder," she said, "about your family heritage. Where did your ancestors come from?"

"We're American from way back."

"I could see you as a baron or something," she said. "His lordship, Adam Briggs."

He scoffed. "More likely Briggs is short for brigand."

"Even better. Your ancestor might have been a romantic highwayman, riding through the night on a dark steed with his cape flying."

"A criminal." He lifted a skeptical eyebrow. "And you find that attractive?"

"There's something appealing about a dashing thief or a pirate who would swoop down and carry me off into his fabulous, mysterious world. A king of the outlaws. And I would be his queen."

"Fairy tales," Adam said disparagingly. "That's the sort of story Amelia would like, except that her hero would be a basset hound."

In her childhood, Molly liked to make up stories that took her away from cold, hard reality. "Come on, Adam. Didn't you ever want to be someone different? Someone exotic?"

"Why?"

"Because the world of dreams is a lot more dramatic than everyday life." She smoothed the folds of his oversize flannel shirt across her lap. "That's one reason why I like to dress up."

"What's the other reason?"

"Because I look good in sequins."

Though he hadn't obviously deflected her questions, the conversation had somehow turned around and was about her. "I want to talk about you for a change."

"Why?"

"Let's say I'm practicing my interrogation skills," she said. "If you couldn't be yourself, who would you want to be?"

He gave a short laugh. "This isn't an interrogation. It's an Oprah interview."

Determinedly, she stuck to her question. "You must have fantasies. Like being a pirate. Or an outlaw. You tell me."

"A judge," he said. "If I could pick another profession. I'd be on the bench."

She sipped her liqueur. The liquid warmth shimmered through her, creating a sense of well-being. "Would you be an off-with-his-head kind of judge?"

"Hell, no."

"You'd follow the rules," she said. "And you'd play fair."

"Always."

But he hadn't played by the rules tonight. When she asked him not to inform the police about the attack, he'd agreed. This was so totally out of character that she still couldn't believe it. She didn't want to probe too deeply into this unusual cooperation. He might change his mind. "If you were a judge, what would you tell me to do next?"

"Quit this investigation," he said quickly. "It's dangerous, and you sure as hell don't owe anything to Pierce, who is probably lying to you."

"I'm afraid it's too late," she said. "I can't quit now. Somebody's trying to kill me."

He visibly winced. "I hate this, Molly."

"Well, I'm not real fond of the idea myself. But it stands to reason that whoever came after me isn't going to give up."

"I agree. We have no choice but to pursue this investigation." He cleared his throat. "However, the increased level of threat requires a somewhat different approach. I need to lay down some ground rules."

"Rules?" She didn't like the sound of this.

"Number one: you go nowhere without me. Number two: you will be armed."

"That doesn't make any sense," she complained. "If you're going to be my bodyguard, why do I have to be armed?"

"I might get taken out," he said.

"What do you mean?"

"Shot, stabbed or otherwise disabled so I can't protect you."

She shuddered at his plainly spoken words. What if her first field investigation resulted in Adam being injured…or even killed. Fate wouldn't be that cruel. "That won't happen."

"A good battle plan prepares for every contingency." He drained the amber liquid from his snifter and returned to the chair opposite her. "I consider it highly unlikely that I'll be incapacitated. When it becomes necessary to kick ass, I'm damn good at it."

Though she had never actually seen Adam in a fist fight or a shoot-out, she didn't doubt his abilities. "I'll bet you are."

"Now, we're going to talk about strategy," he said.

She groaned. "I've heard this lecture before."

"Fine." He leaned back in his chair. "You tell me."

"Whenever possible, use the element of surprise. Strike first, and strike fast."

He nodded. "What else?"

"When you're entering a dangerous situation, always leave yourself an escape route."

"Good," Adam said.

"If you're losing the battle, retreat."

He grinned. "I'm surprised. You actually have been paying attention."

"I just look like a vapid beauty queen." She tapped her forehead. "My mind is a steel trap."

Before he could comment, his attention was diverted and he glanced toward the staircase. "Did you hear something from the guest bedroom?"

She shook her head. "I'm sure Amelia is okay."

But Adam was already on the move, climbing the stairs two at a time.

Though Molly could have stayed put, she set down her snifter and followed him. His home was, of course, equipped with a state-of-the-art security system, and there was no reason to presume anyone would try to break into a second floor window.

She joined Adam as he opened the door to the guest bedroom. The glow from the bedside lamp shone gently on Amelia's blond curls. The covers were tossed aside, and her puppy-patterned pajamas were hiked up to her knees.

Adam went to the bed and leaned over her. Tenderly, he pushed back her bangs and felt the little girl's forehead. Then he pulled the comforter up over her and stepped back. "She seems warm, maybe feverish."

Molly took his place at the bedside and placed a light kiss on Amelia's forehead, inhaling the clean fragrance of baby shampoo. She looked down at the sleeping child. This moment seemed perfect. Sweet and tender. It would be a miracle to have a child of her own, a real family of her own.

She stepped back from the bedside. "No fever."

Together, they tiptoed into the hallway. Adam left the door slightly ajar. The worry lines on his forehead deepened. "Are you sure she's not sick?"

"If she is, there's not much you can do about it." Molly descended the staircase. "Kids pick up all kinds of sniffles and snuffles. It's part of building their little immune systems."

"Not while I'm in charge," he said.

She glanced over her shoulder at him. "What are you going to do? Line up all the germs and blow them away with a bazooka?"

"I might," he said.

As they settled back in the living room, she realized that she'd learned something new about Adam, after all. He was paternal. "You're so different around Amelia."

"No, I'm not."

"Usually, you're this world-weary cynic. A solitary man." She picked up her snifter and finished the Courvoisier. "I always thought that came from your time in the Marines. Seeing so much tragedy and devastation must have made you wary of relationships."

Adam rolled his eyes. "I thought we were done analyzing me."

"You leave me no choice. If you won't tell me what's going on inside your noggin, I have to guess."

He spread his hands wide open. "Okay, Molly. What do you want to know?"

Never before had he invited her questions. "Will you really tell me?"

"Shoot."

She might have asked about the Marine Corps. He'd seen combat and been awarded medals for heroism. But she was even more curious about his boyhood. "Tell me about your parents. I know they retired in Ohio and were married for nearly forty-five years."

"Which was probably forty-four years too long," he said. "They fought. Often."

She frowned. "I always thought you and your sister had an idyllic childhood."

"We moved often. My mother didn't like being uprooted. And my father didn't like when she complained." His eyes seemed to darken as he looked backward into the past. "Far from an idyll."

"Was there a lot of yelling?"

"Some," Adam said.

"What did you do?"

Molly was very familiar with this version of childhood, hiding in closets and waiting for the thunderous noise of an adult argument to pass. She remembered hugging her knees, trying to make herself so small that she was invisible.

She watched Adam, waiting for his response. His lips clamped together. There was a barely perceptible shake of his head, and she could see him pulling back, shutting down.

"Tell me," she said. "When your parents argued—"

"They fought," he said bitterly. "It wasn't a discussion or an interview or even a freaking interrogation. They went at it. Tooth and nail."

"And what did you do?"

"I took care of my baby sister. She was five years younger than me. I took her outside for a walk or I played games with her."

"But you couldn't completely shield her from what was going on."

"No." His reply was terse. "I couldn't protect her."

"You were just a kid," Molly said.

"I should have taken her away from there. Should have found another way for her to grow up."

"You did the best you could."

"Not good enough. By the time my sister was a teenager, she was a mess. Flunking out of high school. Dating idiots. Not taking care of herself."

"I'm sorry."

He glanced toward the staircase. "That's why Amelia is so remarkable. I look at that sweet child, and I realize that my sister is married to a good man. Her life turned out okay."

"What about you?"

"Me? I'm fine. No worries." He stood and stretched. Apparently, he thought this conversation was over. "Time for bed."

"Wait, Adam. I still have more questions about—"

"Tomorrow," he said. "We need sleep. Amelia will be picked up tomorrow at 09:00. And we'll have a full day of investigation. Good night, Molly."

Before she could protest, he pivoted in a crisp military turn and exited up the staircase.

She was left alone with her thoughts. For the first time in her seven years of knowing Adam, she'd seen a glimpse of his vulnerability. Finally, she had an idea of where his intense protectiveness came from.

When they first met, she'd been picking his pocket. He could have turned her over to the police and walked away. But he took her under his wing. In her, he might have seen his sister's plight. Molly had nowhere to turn, no one to help.

No one but Adam.

And how had she repaid him? There was the obvious fact that she worked hard at CCC. Her organizational skills were a definite asset.

But she wanted to do more. She wanted to be the person who turned his life around.

She pushed herself out of the chair and padded across his living room floor. Though she wasn't the world's best interrogator, her intuition was just fine. And she'd learned what was different about Adam.

Being with Amelia caused him to have second thoughts about his own life and the possibility that he might be able to settle down and have a good relationship like his sister. He was a good man, and he deserved it. A loving home and a family.

Maybe she was the woman who could give that to him.

ON THE DESKTOP, the thief arranged three black pens in a row, then in a triangle. It wouldn't be smart to write the note. The police had experts who could trace handwriting back to the author.

He couldn't afford to be caught.

But he couldn't keep this secret. He knew what was going to happen. And he knew when. A great deal of money would change hands—none of it deserved.

Certainly, he had considered the ways he might profit from his knowledge. Blackmail was one. But he despised lying, manipulation and making demands. He was a thief. He worked alone. No one else was endangered by his work. No one was hurt.

It wasn't right for them to get away with this crime. They disgusted him. They thought he was blind, that they could pull off this caper right under his nose.

They were wrong.

He turned to the computer keyboard and typed in all capital letters.

Chapter Ten

Adam spotted the white delivery van. It was parked on the street outside Pierce's townhouse.

He slipped his Land Cruiser into a nearby parking slot. This newly constructed area near downtown Denver was six square blocks of town houses and multistory brick condos with shops on the street level to simulate the neighborhood atmosphere that had been wiped out when the development was built.

Turning to Molly who sat in the passenger seat, Adam asked, "Is that the van your attacker was driving?"

"Could be." She peered through the car window. "How can I know for sure? I mean, a white van? I can hardly tell one regular car from another."

"And yet," he said, "you can spot a Porsche at two hundred yards."

"When it comes to the eighty-thou-and-up cars, I'm an expert. Because I like the good stuff." She arched an eyebrow. "Just like you."

Sure, he appreciated the finer things, but he'd never been impressed by a price tag. Nor was Molly. Though she liked to peg herself as a high-maintenance woman, she wasn't self-absorbed enough to be a diva.

This morning, after Amelia had been picked up by

her mother, they swung by Molly's house so she could change clothes. It took her less than fifteen minutes to grab her notes for the day's investigation and to assemble herself in a fringed purple skirt and a fuzzy red and purple sweater that showed a sexy inch of her flat midriff when she raised her arm.

He'd told her that she didn't look like any field investigator that he'd ever seen. And she responded by hiking up her skirt and pointing to platform shoes that she claimed were good for running fast.

She swung those shoes out of the car and went toward the white van. Slowly, she circled the vehicle. "It's got the same kind of sliding door."

Adam read the license plate number. Might as well check out the ownership. "Did you touch the van last night? Would there be fingerprints?"

As she tried to remember, her forehead tightened in an adorable scowl. In those fifteen minutes of getting dressed, she'd also applied makeup. Her mouth glistened with a moist pink shimmer.

Distracted by the sheen from her lips, he didn't catch what she was saying. "What?"

"I think we should break into the van and see if there's a black ski mask or something."

"No way." He'd already bent the rules as far as he intended.

"But this is a big, fat, hairy clue."

"Or a coincidence."

"Come on, Adam. I know how to slip a wire inside the window to open the lock."

"Why am I not surprised."

After trying the door on the driver's side, she rummaged through her massive purse, looking for a tool to help her break into the white van.

He pulled his cell phone from his pocket. "I'll phone in the plates and find out who owns—"

"Aha!" She yanked on the panel door which slid right open. With no trepidation whatsoever, she climbed inside. "The rear is empty."

"Get the hell out of there, Molly."

"I found a camera," she called out. "Maybe this is Ronald's van."

Her impetuous action annoyed him. In spite of being assaulted last night, she apparently didn't grasp the potential for danger. "Even if we find evidence, we can't use it in an unauthorized search."

"Not true." She stuck her head out of the van door. "That only applies to a police search, and we're not the cops. Besides, we never reported the attack last night, so it really doesn't count."

Her logic was so convoluted that he couldn't frame a response. The attack didn't count? What the hell did that mean? He was beginning to regret his decision to leave the police out of the loop.

"Look!" She held up a crumpled bag from a fast food place. "Do you think we could test the French fry remains for DNA?"

Before he could reply, she disappeared again into the van.

Adam resigned himself to the fact that Molly was making an unauthorized search and that his job was to keep watch. He glanced up and down the tidy sidewalk outside the development. Though hundreds of people lived in this area, few were on the street. It was after ten o'clock in the morning and most of the residents were at work.

Maintaining a lookout, Adam pushed aside his navy-blue blazer for easy access to his sidearm. He was also wearing an ankle holster.

Molly leaped from the van. In her right hand she held a torn envelope. "Evidence," she said.

"Of what?"

"This van belongs to Pierce. There were other documents in the glove compartment."

"That's information I could have gotten with a phone call," he said. "Breaking into the van was unnecessary."

"No harm done."

He pulled the panel door closed, took Molly's arm and led her onto the sidewalk. He kept his voice low, trying to impress upon her the seriousness of the situation. "We're not playing games, Molly. As we proceed with this field investigation, we need to exercise all due caution."

"Okay," she said blithely.

"That means you can't jump into someone's van just because it's sitting here. Do you understand?"

"Sir. Yes, sir." She tossed off a sarcastic salute. "We'll have to ask Pierce who has keys to his van. Obviously, somebody else used it last night."

"We don't even know if this is the same vehicle," he said. "Do you have any idea how many white vans there are in the Denver area?"

"Lots," she said. "But it has to be this one."

"Why?"

"Because there can't be that many white van owners in Denver who want me dead."

"Only because they haven't met you," he muttered under his breath as he led the way toward Pierce's town house.

He toyed with the cell phone, considering whether or not he should call the police. Last night, he'd been blinded by his sympathy for Molly's emotional state and might have made a mistake. Throughout his career with CCC, Adam always cooperated one hundred percent with the proper authorities.

But this case was different. Molly had been threatened. Ted Berringer, the detective in charge of the case, not only seemed disinterested in this investigation but was openly hostile toward Molly.

Adam would stick with his initial judgment. He and Molly would investigate on their own.

As they approached the neatly landscaped stucco town house, he glanced at this sometimes infuriating woman who tended toward risky spontaneity. Her unprofessional behavior had to stop immediately.

She smiled up at him. "This is fun."

"It's dangerous. Your friend, Pierce, was almost murdered."

"But he's going to be okay. The docs said so." She winked. "And I'm just fine."

As they walked up the sidewalk to Pierce's town house, Adam unholstered his Glock automatic. "I go first. You stay back and keep quiet."

"Why?"

"Because we don't know who might be in the condo," he said. "Just do what I say."

She lightly touched his forearm. "Nothing bad is going to happen."

"How do you figure?"

"Because you're with me, and you can be a pretty scary dude when you want to be." She gave his arm a squeeze. "I know you'll protect me from the bad guys."

A totally irrational feeling of pride swelled inside his chest. She trusted him. She believed in him. How had his ethics gotten so twisted that her opinion mattered more than following the proper procedure?

Gun in hand, Adam unlocked the door. He pushed it

wide. Before stepping inside, he paused and listened. There were sounds from within. Someone was here.

He gestured for Molly to stay back.

"What's going on?" she asked.

"Quiet, Molly."

"Okay. Sorry."

From inside the condo came a female voice. "Who's there?"

Adam shrugged. "So much for the element of surprise."

Molly brushed past him and called out, "Is that you, Gloria?"

"Who is it?" Gloria Vanderly strode into the living room as if she owned the place. "What are you two doing here?"

Adam subtly slipped his gun back into the holster. "We might ask you the same question, ma'am."

"I used to live here," she snapped.

"But not anymore." Adam felt a lot more comfortable confronting Gloria in this masculine town house with leather sofas and football trophies. Yesterday, at her bridal boutique, he'd been strangling in bridal veils. "Why are you here?"

"Not that it's any of your business," Gloria said, "but I dropped by on my way to the hospital so I could pick something up."

"What would that be?"

Her eyes flicked down and to the left as she searched for a lie. "A book of poetry. Pierce wanted me to read to him."

"Are you telling me that a former Denver Bronco wants poems?"

"I can't find the book anyway." She glanced at her wristwatch. "I'm late."

Adam blocked her path to the exit. "What are you driving this morning, Gloria?"

She pulled her head back like a turtle going into its shell. "I have a black Mercedes."

He carefully observed her reaction as he asked, "Do you ever use Pierce's white delivery van?"

"Not unless it's necessary." Her dark eyes confronted him in blatant challenge.

"But you have keys."

"I suppose so."

"Last night," he said. "Did you use the van?"

"No." She called over her shoulder. "Let's go, Denny."

Denny Devlin, the caterer, appeared from the hallway. Sheepishly, he ran his hand through his curly brown hair. His attitude reminded Adam of a lover caught in the act. As he approached Molly, he pulled up a grin.

She smiled back. "Nice to see you again, Denny. We should talk about the menu for Heidi's wedding this weekend."

He glanced at Gloria, then back at Molly. "Why are you interested in Heidi's wedding?"

"I'm surprised Gloria didn't tell you," Molly said. "I'm running Pierce's business while he's in the hospital."

"Is there a problem with the catering?" he asked.

"Not as far as I know."

"Good. Because this is a very important job for me."

"Why?" Molly asked.

"It's the Brown Palace." He spoke the name of the hotel with reverence. "Lots of important people will be there. I want to make an impression."

When Denny and Gloria stood side by side, they

could have been brother and sister. They were the same height. The same lean build. Either one of them fit the description for the person who attacked Molly.

"You two are friendly," Adam said.

"It's only natural," Gloria replied coldly. "We both work in the same field."

"And you both feel free to enter Pierce's home when he isn't here."

"That's the way it is with friends." Gloria tucked her leather briefcase under her arm and stalked past him toward the exit. "We have to run."

From what? Adam doubted that these two suspects were together for innocent reasons. They had the look of coconspirators. He remembered the scenario he and Molly had created for the attack on Pierce. One person was talking to him. Another stabbed him in the back. Gloria and Denny fit the bill.

When the door closed behind them, he flipped the dead bolt and fastened the chain. "Those two are up to something."

He went toward the hallway where Denny had been lurking. There were two bedrooms and a den with a desk, bookcases and a television set.

Molly slipped behind the desk and sat in the chair. She pulled open the bottom drawer and rifled through the files with efficient expertise. "This seems to be mostly personal financial stuff. Why would Gloria be looking in here?"

"Didn't you tell me that Pierce and Gloria had given a substantial loan to Denny Devlin?"

"Right," Molly said. She flipped her fingernails across the colored tabs on the hanging file folders. "Something's missing. There's a file missing."

"How do you know?"

"Don't you remember? Pierce and I met at a class on how to organize your business. We both use an identical filing and coding system."

From the front of the drawer, she pulled out a ledger and scanned the pages with a lightning speed that never failed to amaze Adam. Though Molly was capable of flaky behavior, she was a total ace when it came to administrative work.

Leaning back in the desk chair, she clucked her tongue and frowned. "The missing file folder pertains to a loft that Pierce owns in downtown Denver. It's a real classy place. I went there once for a party."

"And why would Gloria take that file?"

She drew the obvious conclusion. "There's something at that loft she doesn't want us to see."

MOLLY'S MIND RACED as they drove to their midday appointment with Ronald Atchison. What could Gloria be hiding at Pierce's loft? Possibly the missing items from the magpie thefts. But that didn't make sense; none of the stolen objects were especially valuable. Why bother hiding them?

"Maybe Gloria is a fence," she said. "Selling stolen goods."

"She makes plenty of dough at her boutique," Adam said. "I think we should be looking at Denny Devlin."

"What could he be hiding?"

"Not sure. Think about his business."

She visualized Denny's shop with the kitchen where he did his cooking. A lot of that equipment was expensive, but she really didn't think he'd be stashing bread mixers and pizza ovens in Pierce's downtown loft.

It had to be something easily transported—something simple. A lightbulb went on inside her head. "Oh my God! I think I've got it. He's hiding people. Illegal immigrants."

"Possible," Adam said.

Denny's catering business relied on low-wage work-ers—cooks, servers and delivery people. He might have nefarious connections through his employees. "But ev-erybody who works for him is bonded."

"That wasn't always the case. He was careless enough in his hiring to take on an employee with hepatitis."

A people-smuggling business? She frowned. Some-thing about her idea didn't ring true. Pierce's loft was in a fancy, high-rent building. Surely, the other residents would notice if mobs of aliens came shuffling through.

Maybe there weren't mobs. Maybe it was only one or two important immigrants. People who needed to slip into town under the radar. "Terrorists," she concluded enthusiastically. "Denny Devlin is running an under-cover terrorist operation."

Adam gave her one of those looks—a sidelong glance that measured her sanity and found her a few cups short of a gallon. "He's a chef, Molly. His expert-ise is hot cookies and cheese puffs."

"Which is why it's a perfect cover," she said. "No-body would suspect a wedding caterer of international espionage. That's just about as likely as me being en-gaged to a wealthy Australian kangaroo farmer."

"Which you're not," Adam pointed out.

"But I could be."

She might not have all the loose ends tied together, but her conclusion was right on target. The loft was being used to hide people—important people who needed to come and go without leaving a trace. If they weren't terrorists, who were they? And how were they connected to the wedding business?

Adam said, "When you were attacked last night, you said that you injured your assailant."

"Right."

"Did you notice if Denny or Gloria were limping?"

"They weren't." That was the first thing she looked for. "But Denny gave me a weird look. As if we shared some kind of secret."

Adam parked on the street in front of a quaint adobe-style church where she had arranged to meet Ronald Atchison.

"We're here," he said. "What's our interest in Ronald?"

"He was at all the weddings where there were thefts."

"He took photos?" Adam asked.

She nodded. "I asked him to bring some along. Also, he's the only suspect who has a criminal record."

"For what?"

"Fraud. And he's been charged with other white-collar crimes. When I talked to him on the phone, he suggested that Pierce was attacked because of the money, honey."

"He calls you honey?"

"I've met him once or twice," she said. "He likes the way I dress."

They entered the church through a heavy wooden door. The pale adobe walls contrasted with an arched ceiling and wooden beams. Light filtered gently through several stained glass windows, creating a serene golden glow.

Molly felt herself smiling. Though she wasn't a particularly religious person, she always found peace within the walls of a sanctuary. A church was a haven— a place she could think, a place she could go when all other doors were closed.

Ronald strode up the center aisle between the pews.

"Your timing is excellent. I've just completed this shoot and packed up my equipment."

He gave Molly a hug, then admired her engagement ring. After shaking hands with Adam, Ronald got right down to business. "First thing," he said. "You need an engagement photo for the newspapers. You'll want to bring your sweetie along."

Though Molly had no intention of posing, she played along. "What kind of picture would you suggest?"

He eyeballed her up and down, reaching over to adjust the line of her sweater. "You don't need the standard glamor photo makeup, Miss Molly. I could get creative with you."

"How so?"

"We could do something outdoorsy with the wind in your hair."

As he studied her intently, his eyes became dark and penetrating. "Step back," he said. "Put down the purse and hold your arms out."

She did as he asked.

"Turn," he said. "Slowly."

When she completed a three-sixty, he gave her a hug, a smile and a wink. Ronald was gorgeous—tall, dark and handsome. His features were perfect, and Molly envied his silky skin tone, which was, no doubt, the result of careful, constant moisturizing. Gay guys really knew how to take care of themselves.

"I have a crazy idea," he said. "Your hubby-to-be might go for some suggestive poses."

"For the newspaper?" Adam said gruffly.

"Of course not," Ronald said. "But Molly's fiancé might want special pictures for his private use."

Adam's upper lip curled in a snarl. "Are you talking about porn?"

"Don't get your panties in a knot," Ronald said. "I'm always tasteful. But most of the brides who come to me aren't very inspiring. Molly's different. I mean, look at her! She's got the bod of Miss September without the airbrushing."

Though Adam didn't like this guy with all his touching and over-the-top enthusiasm, he had to agree with his appreciation of Molly. She was a beautiful woman.

"It might help," she said, "if I could take a look at some other photos. Did you bring along the samples I asked for?"

"The Deitrich wedding," he said. "I have the pictures outside in my van."

Before they even left the church, Adam knew what they'd find parked outside on the street. Another plain white van with a sliding panel door.

Chapter Eleven

Adam stared at the white delivery van, and he recalled his earlier conversation with Molly. How many people who owned white vans wanted to kill her?

Apparently, there was a whole damned fleet of them.

Until now, he'd considered Ronald Atchison to be a marginal suspect, but the van made a difference. Also, Ronald was the same tall, lean body type as Gloria and Denny—the same type as the person who attacked Molly.

Ronald yanked open the side panel door. Adam noted that the interior of the van was crammed with lighting equipment and cameras. Though Molly hadn't mentioned seeing anything inside the van, he was learning not to put much stock in what she'd said. Molly was efficient and quick-thinking, but she was possibly the world's most unreliable witness.

Adam would have to probe for other incriminating evidence to validate his suspicion of Ronald. It was hard to get an accurate reading on this touchy-feely guy who couldn't keep his hands off Molly when he talked.

What were the facts? Ronald, the wedding photographer, lived beyond his means. He'd been in prison for fraud. He was slick and good-looking. Wore a Cartier wristwatch and a gold chain around his neck.

With him, Adam assumed that money was the prime motivator. He asked, "Does Pierce send a lot of business your way?"

"Not as much as he could," Ronald said.

"What about Gloria?"

"Don't get me started on Gloria, the Wicked Witch of the West. She always wants full-length photos to show off her gowns."

"What's wrong with that?" Molly asked.

"Oh, please." He flapped his hands and teasingly patted her shoulder. "Imagine a hefty bride. Swaddled in glaring white. Trust me, sweetie. It's not a pretty picture."

"All brides are beautiful," Molly said staunchly.

"In their dreams," he said.

"That's right." She appeared to be getting angry. "Every bride has a special aura that makes them fantastic. It's magical."

"You're quite the romantic," Ronald said. "Actually, I agree. When I'm working with a bride who's never going to be a cover girl, that's what I go for. The dreamy look. Maybe a tight focus on the eyes. Or her hand with the wedding ring." He reached over and took Molly's hand. "My point is, Gloria's gowns aren't always the most important thing."

Adam said, "You and Gloria don't get along."

"But of course we do." He seemed to take offense. "We're professionals. I need her, and she needs me. We've known each other for ages."

"As long as you've known Pierce?"

"At least."

Molly spoke up, "Do you remember that loft Pierce has downtown? We met at a party there?"

"Well, sure." He released Molly's hand. "But don't ask for details. If I could remember every party I went to, there wouldn't be room in my head for anything else."

Was he covering up? Adam couldn't tell. Ronald was glib; he put on a good show with his constant chatter. Now, it was time for Adam to throw down the gauntlet and see what this guy responded to. "You're an intense person, Ronald."

"Thanks, I think."

"Emotional," Adam said. "Passionate. Maybe even temperamental."

"Dear me, yes. I'm an artist."

"When your temper gets out of control," Adam said, "somebody might get hurt."

"What do you mean?"

"Crime of passion."

For a moment, Ronald's la-di-da attitude was eclipsed by a flash of hostility. His shoulders tensed. The gleam in his eyes flattened to a cold opaque darkness. He was wary, and Adam knew he'd struck a chord. "Tell me about your relationship with Pierce."

"No real relationship. It's all about money." Ronald struck a studied pose, hiding again behind his chatty persona. "Now I know who you are. Molly's boss. The director of Colorado Crime Consultants."

"That's right."

"Love your work," Ronald said with fake enthusiasm. "You were involved with catching that serial killer, the one who arranged all his victims like mermaids. And, of course, the Carrington affair with that poor girl who hid out in the woods for a month."

"You did photos at the Carrington wedding," Molly said. "But I didn't see you there."

"Honey, when I'm working, I'm invisible."

"You? That's hard to believe."

"I fade into the woodwork. Nobody notices me at all. But that wasn't the case at the Carrington wedding. I didn't do candids at that reception."

"This weekend," she said, "you'll be doing candids at the Brown Palace wedding."

"That's what it says in my contract." He reached into his van, pulled out an eight-by-ten brown envelope and handed it to her. "Here are the pictures for the Deitrich wedding reception. The ones you wanted. Now, I really have to run."

When Ronald tried to pull the van door closed, Adam braced his hand against it. He wasn't ready to let this guy off the hook. "I heard you were in prison."

"That's right," Ronald said. "I paid my debt to society."

"Do you keep in touch with your old inmates?"

"Only if they're getting married," Ronald said.

"Because then they would pay you. It's all about money."

"Makes the world go around." Ronald twirled his finger in a circle.

"A professional photographer has other skills," Adam said. "You could make phony IDs. Passports. Maybe even try your hand at counterfeiting."

"Not my style."

Style was an important consideration. The person who attacked Pierce and Molly used a knife. Not a gun. Not their fists.

Forensic profilers had told Adam that knives were most often the weapon of choice for women. Assault with a blade was more personal. "When you were in prison," Adam said, "did you learn to handle a shiv?"

"If you're referring to some sort of handmade blade, I think not. I'm a lover, not a fighter."

"And you're an artist," Adam said. "A temperamental artist with marketable criminal talents."

He could see the rage building in Ronald. His smooth complexion flushed red. He blinked rapidly. When he tried a dismissive chuckle, the sound was brittle. "I really must go."

Not without a final warning. "You know my reputation," Adam said. "CCC has a high rate of success in closing cases."

"So I've heard."

"You should also hear this. Molly is under my protection. Come after her, and you'll be dealing with me."

Adam stepped away from the van, allowing Ronald to slide the panel door shut. Stiffly, the handsome photographer circled around his van to the driver's side door.

"See you this weekend at the Brown Palace wedding," Molly called out.

Ronald paused. Staring at Molly, he took a breath as if he were about to say something important. Then his lips clamped shut.

Molly asked, "Ronald, is there something you wanted to tell me."

"It's nothing." He waved farewell and got into his van. "Ta, sweetie."

As he drove away, Molly came toward Adam. He expected her to be ticked off about the way he'd treated this guy who lavished compliments on her. Instead, she said, "You saw something dangerous in Ronald."

"Sure, I did. Anybody who's been in jail needs a second look. Besides, he's on your short list of suspects."

"That's just on paper. And that was when I was think-ing about the magpie thefts. I could see Ronald swip-ing a couple of shiny objects, almost as a joke. But stabbing Pierce in the back?"

"Given the right motivation," he said, "anybody is capable of violence."

"Ronald couldn't have come after me last night be-cause I talked to him on the phone right before I left the office and went into the parking lot."

"Cell phone," Adam pointed out. "Call forwarding."

"I didn't think of that. He could have been on his cell phone, sitting outside the building. Waiting. Lurking." She stamped her foot. "Why didn't that occur to me? Why am I so bad at reading people?"

Adam saw two answers. The first was a positive qual-ity: her tendency to see the good in others. The second was annoying. "You can't read Ronald because you like him."

"True."

Adam thought that if he were more like Ronald, he'd have reached out and patted her shoulder. He'd pull her into his arms and gently stroke her shoulders, comfort-ing her. But he'd never been a hands-on guy. Those who invaded his personal space were more likely to re-ceive a karate chop to the throat than a hug. He kept his distance, even from Molly.

"I really do like Ronald," she said.

Inwardly, he snarled. But he kept his voice calm. "I can see that."

"I'd love to see him when he's all dolled up in his drag queen outfit. I'll bet he's spectacular."

"He's gay?"

"Duh." She started toward his car then suddenly halted and threw up her hands. "I can't believe this. I left my purse in the church."

Ronald was gay. He wasn't a threat…at least not in the sense Adam expected. The handsome Ronald wasn't somebody Molly would date unless she wanted to compare wardrobes.

"Are you sure he's gay?" Adam asked as he held open the wooden door to the church. "He wants you to come in for a sitting to do porn photos."

"Artsy baloney," she said.

Inside the quiet sanctuary, she grabbed her purse from a back pew, slung the strap over her shoulder and turned toward the altar. For a moment, she stood quietly.

Adam stepped up beside her. He thought of placing his arm around her waist. Behind her back, he reached out. Then his hand dropped. If he touched her once, he wouldn't be able to stop.

"This is a pretty church," she said. "Simple. It would be a nice place for my wedding if I was really getting married."

The wistful tone in her voice kept him from making a snide comment about fake fiancés and undercover brides. During the past few days, he'd come to realize that all this wedding madness held a bizarre grip on women—all women, including Molly who was usually down-to-earth. When she talked about the ceremony and the dress and all that other stuff, her eyes glazed over and she fell into a trance state.

She took a graceful step down the center aisle between the pews. "I've been doing all this research on weddings. People spend thousands of dollars decorating the church with flowers and ribbons. Sometimes, live trees."

What a waste! But Adam held his tongue.

She took another step. "I think I'd like roses in my bouquet. Or maybe lilies."

Her chin lifted as she gazed toward the simple altar. Light from the stained glass windows shone gently upon her face. "When I tried on that gown at Gloria's boutique, I felt amazing. Special."

Adam realized that he was walking beside her, making an impromptu march down the aisle. Wasn't this the traditional position of the father of the bride? The man who would give Molly away?

Damn it, that wasn't his job. If anybody was going to marry Molly, it was him. He stepped in front of her, unable to hold his silence for one more moment. "It's all a show. All these preparations. The roses. The gowns. The fancy little sandwiches. What difference does it make? The most expensive wedding ceremony in the world can't guarantee a good marriage."

"How would you know?" Molly shot back. "You're like me. Married once, too young. And it was a mess."

"I know what it takes to have a good relationship," he said. "Mutual respect. Tolerance. Good conversation."

"You're talking about a partnership," she said.

"You're right." That was the relationship he'd had with her. Partners. Co-workers.

"And you're forgetting the most important thing about a marriage."

Her blue eyes sparkled as she looked up at him. He knew her face as well as he knew his own. Almost every day for seven years, he'd seen that face. That smile. That dimple at the corner of her full lips.

He knew she was a beautiful woman. Yet he'd never been affected by her charms until she'd been in danger and he realized he might lose her. He couldn't imagine his life without Molly. *Tell her. Let her know how much she means to you.*

Standing here, in the center of this peaceful church, he was racked with inner turmoil. His heartbeat accelerated. His blood raced through his veins. He was dizzy with the need to touch her.

"Love," she said softly. "The most important part of a true marriage is love."

Unable to resist, he leaned toward her. His intention was to kiss her forehead, to ease gently into what might be a new phase in their partnership. As he drew closer, he couldn't hold back. She was too tempting, too enticing. His arms encircled her. His mouth claimed hers.

Time stopped. Adam was transported as he pulled her close. No longer thinking of what was right and prudent, he gave himself entirely to their kiss.

Beneath the fuzzy texture of her purple and red striped sweater, he felt her slender, supple body. Her sweet softness aroused him. He'd been waiting for this moment. Perhaps all his life.

Her arms tightened around him, encouraging him. Though his shoulder holster got in the way, she pressed tightly against him, and he knew that she wanted this closeness as much as he did.

Her lips parted. Her tongue met his as he penetrated through her teeth to the satin interior of her mouth. *Oh, Molly. Why did I wait so long?*

MOLLY CLUNG to him. Her eyes were closed. Her knees were weak. *Why had he waited so long for this kiss?* For seven years, she'd known Adam—a very long time for the sexual tension to build. And she hadn't even been aware of it. She'd been unconsciously holding her breath, waiting to exhale.

She moved her body against him, loving the way his wiry, muscular length fit perfectly with her. The way he held her showed his strength and authority. Adam always did everything well. Even a kiss.

When she felt him pulling away, she tightened her grasp. She didn't want this moment to end. She wanted to go on kissing him for all eternity.

His lips separated from hers. *No! Not yet!*

She kept her eyes closed, afraid to open them and face him. Would he look different to her? Would she see regret in his eyes? Had this kiss been a mistake?

"Molly?" His deep baritone voice was a caress. "Are you all right?"

She nodded. The first words that she spoke to him after this life-changing kiss ought to be significant.

He asked, "Do you want to sit down?"

In the back of her mind, she remembered that they were in a church. She ought to kneel in the pew and offer thanks for this unexpected blessing. Was that sacrilegious? Maybe so. She wasn't thinking clearly.

Her eyelids pried open, and she gazed full into his face. His features hadn't changed. But everything was different. Her perception of him was more finely tuned. She could read his emotions. He was excited. And doubtful. And cautious.

Not knowing what to say, she stepped away from his embrace. Her throat tightened. She couldn't swallow. For Pete's sake, this was Adam! How could she feel uncomfortable around him?

"Possibly," he said, "I might have chosen a better venue for this moment."

"Really?" Her tone was flippant. Her comment was pure reflex. "Are you telling me that making out in a church isn't your style?"

"Not as a rule."

"You be sure to give me a copy of that particular

rule book. The one with proper venues for red-hot kisses."

She bit her tongue. Molly hadn't wanted to be snippy. She should have found something meaningful to say.

"Red-hot?"

"Totally steamy," she said.

"Then I can assume that it was good for you."

He was smiling. His blue eyes twinkled. It almost seemed as if they had slipped back into their regular pattern, that the kiss never happened. "We should go. We have a lot to do today."

She stalked toward the door and flung it open. Outside, the midday sunlight shone warmly on the faded grass. The crisp autumn breeze combed through her hair. The birds and squirrels still twittered in the treetops.

It was the same old world. But she knew in her heart that everything was different. Immeasurably so.

Chapter Twelve

On the car ride to the hospital to visit Pierce, Molly chatted desperately. She read the road signs and pointed out obvious views and commented endlessly about the weather. Was it hot? Was it cold? When did Adam think the first snow would come?

She even turned on the car radio and sang along. It was necessary, absolutely necessary, to fill the air space between her and Adam with trivia so she wouldn't have to face the true meaning of their kiss.

By the time they reached the hospital, she had run out of diversions. In the middle of the lobby, where patients sat waiting in rows of chairs and personnel in scrubs hurried toward important destinations, she came to a dead halt. "Adam, we need to talk about that kiss."

He arched an eyebrow. His gaze was cool. "Go ahead."

Where to start? "Our working relationship," she said. "It's good. Right? We complement each other. We're professionals. And I don't want to lose that."

"Me, neither."

"Excellent." They were on the same page. "Therefore, I think we should forget that kiss ever happened. Erase it."

"If that's what you want," he said.

But his eyes had begun to heat up. He drew her toward him like a hapless moth to a hundred-watt bulb.

She gestured helplessly. "I mean, I have other things to worry about."

"Like figuring out who attacked Pierce."

"You bet."

"And the fact that someone wants to kill you."

"That, too." Her priorities were seriously out of whack; she was more concerned about a kiss than mortal danger. Loss of life seemed less important than a broken heart.

"I understand, Molly."

"We will never speak of that kiss again." She stuck out her hand. "Shake on it."

As soon as she touched his hand, her resolve washed away in a crashing tidal wave of unexpected emotion. Spontaneous excitement churned and eddied inside her.

Before she knew what she was doing, she'd flung her arm around his neck. She was kissing him! Again!

This was wrong, wrong, wrong.

But it felt so good, good, good.

The hustle and bustle of the hospital faded away, and she was aware only of him. He clasped her waist and pulled her closer. Her body fitted against his like a hand in a smooth leather glove.

Reluctantly, she loosened her grip. She broke away from him and took a step backward. She was happy and excited and humiliated all at the same time. "Apparently, I need to work on impulse control."

"Not on my account," Adam said. "Anytime you want to kiss me, go right ahead."

This certainly hadn't turned out the way she expected. Now what? She remembered one of his strategies: when you're in a situation you can't win, retreat. "I'm going to the ladies' room."

Following the signs, she fled to the public bathroom. Dodging around a mother washing her daughter's hands, Molly went into a stall and locked the door behind her. The inside of her head throbbed from all her chatter. *And then she'd kissed him.*

Quite obviously, she was insane. There was no way Adam could have romantic feelings for her. She'd always known that he liked her...*but not that way.* They were friends. Partners. Adam was her boss, her mentor, the guy who put her on the straight and narrow, the man whose respect she was always trying to earn.

Sure, she'd imagined what it would be like to be Adam's mate. But she wasn't his Eve, and they didn't live in Eden. Such a relationship was impossible. They were too different.

She was a former street kid—a screwup who got an undeniable thrill from picking pockets. She loved flash and excitement and parties.

Adam was an introvert. He lived at the opposite end of the spectrum. His attitudes gave new meaning to the word "rigid." He followed every prescribed regulation and made up new rules for situations when they didn't exist. He was punctual to the second, utterly controlled, competent, reliable...but not boring. Never boring. He had a wry sense of humor, and she knew—above all—that she could count on him. He'd never let her down. He was a good man. The best.

She dragged out a sheet of toilet paper and blew her nose. Good grief, she couldn't start crying. Tears would make everything worse. *Oh, God! Pull yourself together, Molly.*

She left the stall and went to the mirror. There were

three other women in the public bathroom, washing their hands and checking their reflections. Molly set her purse on the sink and opened it. What she needed was lipstick. If she put on a fresh new face, she might find her self-respect.

At the top of her purse was a sheet of white paper, folded twice to letter size. It hadn't been there before. Though her purse was large, the contents were well organized.

She opened the paper and read the typed note, all in capital letters. "DANGER. DANGER. DANGER. THE CRIME IS SET. SATURDAY PM."

Today was Thursday. Heidi's wedding was Saturday.

Molly's hand trembled and the paper fluttered. This note was the answer she'd been waiting for. Something bad was going to happen. And she knew when.

She tore out of the bathroom. Across the crowded hospital lobby, she spotted Adam leaning against a marble column. He was an island of calm in the nervous hospital atmosphere.

She raced up to him, waving the note. "I found this. In my purse."

As he took the paper and read the warning, his expression hardened. His gaze lifted, and he scanned the lobby. "We need to tell Detective Berringer about this."

"I agree." The note was typed on plain white paper—impossible to trace. "There might be fingerprints."

"Unlikely. This was a planned, purposeful warning. The person who slipped the note in your purse would be smart enough to wear gloves." His manner was strictly business. Gone was the gentle manner of the man who had kissed her. Gone was the glow. "When was the last time you looked in your purse?"

"Not since early this morning."

"Think, Molly. Who gave you this note?"

They'd had a busy day, starting at Pierce's town house where they confronted Gloria and Denny Devlin. Then, they'd talked to Ronald. "It could be anybody," she said. "I left my purse unguarded in the church."

He refolded the note and filed it in his inner jacket pocket. "We'll go upstairs and talk to Pierce. Then, we make an appointment with Berringer."

"Right."

She walked beside him toward the elevators. Though the anonymous note held all kinds of scary portent, Molly was grateful to have received tangible proof that a crime was about to be committed. Saturday afternoon or evening. At the time of Heidi's wedding.

Also, the note caused her relationship with Adam to swing back to familiar ground. They were no longer people who had kissed. They were partners.

Confidently, she said, "Here's my game plan with Pierce. The first thing is to see if he's over his alleged amnesia about who stabbed him. We need to find out if he's been talking to anyone else."

Adam nodded. "You should also tell him that you were attacked. If he's half a man, he'll feel guilty enough to explain what the hell is going on."

"Half a man? Pierce is a big guy." She grinned up at Adam as they boarded the elevator. "Not that size matters."

He didn't crack a smile. The thing Adam did best was stay on focus. "What else?"

"We also want to find out why Gloria is so interested in his downtown loft."

When she and Adam entered Pierce's private hospital room, they were immediately confronted by bridal insanity. Heidi, the munchkin-sized bride, flitted back and forth at the foot of Pierce's bed, totally oblivious to the IV and the various hospital monitors. She was dressed in full wedding regalia and had brought Gloria's tailor, Stan Lansky, with her.

"I can't decide," she wailed. "The antique necklace from Smythe Jewelry is so glittery that it seems like I need more sparkle in the gown."

Propped up on his bed pillows, Pierce looked a thousand times better than yesterday. Instead of the standard hospital gown, he wore black silk pajamas. He raised the arm without an IV to wave. "Molly. Adam. You know Heidi."

She rushed at them. Under the frothy gown, her little legs were churning. "You've got to help me, Molly."

A sedative might be useful. Molly wondered if she could get a dose of whatever painkiller was dripping into Pierce's bloodstream. His attitude was positively serene. "How can I help?"

"The necklace," Heidi said, "might overpower the gown. I need something more on the dress, but I don't want to add too much."

"Honey, there's no such thing as too much sparkle. You're the bride. It's your day. Go ahead and light up the ceremony."

"Easy for you to say. You're tall and willowy." She gestured for Stan Lansky to come closer. "Show Molly what the gown would look like with a sequin belt."

The long-suffering tailor dug into a bag of sewing supplies to produce a string of sparkles, which he draped at Heidi's midsection.

"Nice," Molly said. "It calls attention to your tiny little waist. Don't you think so, Adam?"

Though he wasn't listening, Adam managed a nod.

Right at this moment, he was surrounded by his most unfavorite things: feminine lacy stuff and a hospital atmosphere. Yet, he wasn't depressed. His spirits had been permanently elevated by Molly's impromptu kiss in the lobby, and he had a warm feeling near his heart. Nonetheless, he didn't want to be stuck in this room any longer than absolutely necessary.

While Molly and Stan fussed with Heidi's dress, Adam went to Pierce's bedside. "You look better," he said.

"I'm okay. I had worse injuries when I was playing football. Busted knee. Sprained ankles. Cracked ribs. One time when I was skiing, I got a separated shoulder. That hurt like hell." He shrugged. "You know what they say?"

"What?"

"Whatever doesn't kill you makes you stronger."

Though Adam respected his fortitude, this statement didn't bode well for an investigation. Pierce had gone into battle mode—strong and stoic like a soldier. If he had resolved to protect someone, he'd be hard to break.

Adam's words were direct. "But you know this isn't a game. There's no referee. No flag on the play. No rules. Somebody tried to kill you. What if they come after you again?"

"I'll be ready for them." He attempted a grin that slid right off his face. "I'm hoping I can go home tomorrow or the next day."

That diagnosis was maybe a little too optimistic. Pierce's eyes had the dazed look of someone who was buzzed on pain meds.

"It's good to hear you're recovering," Adam said. "Do you remember who stabbed you in the back?"

"Still a blank." He shifted his position on the pillows.

"I've been thinking, Adam. Probably I'll be okay to handle Heidi's wedding this weekend. Molly doesn't have to be involved."

Adam glanced over his shoulder at Stan Lansky. The tailor worked for Gloria and would likely report back to her with anything he overheard. Lowering his voice, Adam said, "Molly's already involved. She was attacked last night."

Pierce's gaze came into focus. He sat up straighter on the bed. "What happened?"

"They waited for her in the parking lot," Adam said quietly. "Jumped out of a white delivery van. Came at her with a knife."

"Damn," Pierce muttered. "I've got a white delivery van. Somebody could have used it."

"Who's got keys?"

"Way too many people. Gloria. Denny Devlin. A couple of florists. I use the van as an all-purpose transport for wedding stuff."

The effort of sitting up was too much for him, and he fell back against the pillows. He was breathing harder, almost gasping. His throat and cheeks had taken on an unhealthy redness.

Adam knew he didn't have much time before Pierce conked out. "Talk to me," he said. "Come on, Pierce. Tell me what's really going on."

"Weddings," he said. "Lots of weddings. Brides. Guys in tuxedos. It's all real pretty. You'd never think…"

"Of crime," Adam said, remembering the note. "You'd never think of a crime being committed at a wedding."

"Never ever." His mind was drifting.

"What's the crime?" Adam asked.

"Don't know."

"What happens on Saturday afternoon?"

"Saturday," he repeated. "When is Saturday?"

"Pierce!" Adam leaned close. "You've got to focus. You don't want Molly to be in danger."

"That's the last thing I want." Suddenly, this big strong guy was on the verge of tears. "I love Molly. She's amazing."

"I know," Adam said. "That's why you've got to talk to me. Tell me who attacked you."

Pierce shook his head. His eyes closed, and he shivered from head to toe. A monitor beside his bed started a loud beeping.

Aware that he was running out of time, Adam applied more pressure. "If you can't tell me who, tell me why. Why did they come after you? Why attack Molly?"

"Can't say." He was sinking into unconsciousness. "Lot of money. Millions. Too much glitter."

Was he talking about Heidi? Or the reason for his attack? "Diamonds?" Adam asked.

"Bad people. Evil."

"Who?" Adam wanted to shake the truth out of him. "Who are the evil people?"

"Killers. Don't let them hurt her. I love her."

"Molly?"

"Sweet Molly."

A red-haired nurse in blue patterned scrubs came into the room and went directly to Pierce. She turned off the beeping monitor and adjusted a band fastened to his arm. "This is too much excitement for you."

"It's okay," Pierce murmured. "I'm fine."

The nurse ignored him. Turning to the other people in the room, she clapped her hands to get their attention. "Visiting time is over."

While Heidi voiced several chirpy objections, Adam leaned close to Pierce's ear. "You own a loft in downtown Denver."

"Yeah."

"What goes on there?"

His eyes opened to slits. "Leased. I get. A rent check. In the mail."

Before Adam could probe for more details, the nurse confronted him. "I'm sorry, sir. You have to leave."

He understood the rules, but this was damn inconvenient. Pierce knew who was behind the attacks. With a little more time and a lot less painkiller, he might open up.

In the corridor, Adam stood by as Molly spoke in quiet, serious tones to the red-haired nurse. Somehow, he had to make sense of Pierce's disjointed comments. He'd spoken of evil people. Though Adam wasn't fond of Denny Devlin or Gloria or Ronald, he wouldn't describe them as evil. Likely, there were other people involved. People who were far more dangerous.

It made sense. One of these people who provided wedding services had gotten involved in a criminal scheme. With real criminals. Evil people.

Maybe Pierce had figured it out. And gotten stabbed for his trouble.

And what about the glitter that Pierce had mentioned? Diamonds? That was the arena of Lucien Smythe, the jeweler.

Molly came up to him. "Pierce is okay. Just exhausted. What did he tell you?"

"Later."

She turned back toward Heidi and Stan, neither of whom seemed to be concerned about Pierce or anything else but the dress.

With a bright smile, Molly said, "Okay, Heidi. Have we got it right? Just a little bit of sparkle on the dress?"

Her head bobbed up and down. She pointed to various spots on her gown. "Here. And here."

"Excuse me," Stan said. "I need to make notes. Does anyone have a pen?"

Molly reached into her purse, quickly finding a pen and a notepad. "Here you go."

The three of them huddled over the notepad, discussing the placement of reflective glass beading on the gown.

"It'll look like raindrops," Molly said. "Or the first snowfall of winter."

"That's a great idea." Heidi beamed. "I'll look like a snow princess."

"These bits of sparkle will balance out the antique necklace," Molly said. "But those diamonds at your throat will draw attention to your pretty face."

"You should be a designer," Heidi gushed.

"I've got style," Molly said. She turned to Stan. "What do you think? Should I be a designer?"

"You couldn't do worse than some of the gowns I've seen." He continued to make notes on the pad. "The bridal business is the place for dramatic style."

Adam really couldn't stand much more of this fluffy nonsense. He clenched his jaw, and his rear molars ground together. He honestly believed everything he'd said to Molly in the church. A fancy wedding didn't guarantee a good marriage.

As far as Adam was concerned, the bride could be wrapped in a bedsheet. Actually, he liked that idea. He stole a glance at Molly, imagining her wearing nothing but a sheet. A nice thought.

Bubbling over with sheer delight, Heidi said, "With these alterations, I'll have a one-of-a-kind dress."

"And you'll be fantastic." Molly turned to the tailor. "Do you have everything you need, Stan?"

He tore off the top sheet of the notepad and handed it back to her. "I'm all set. Heidi and I should get back to the boutique. I have a lot of work to do on this dress before Saturday."

Heidi grasped Molly's hand. "I'm so glad you're taking care of things at the wedding."

"That's my job," Molly said. "Actually, it's Pierce's job. But I'm happy to step in."

Heidi and Stan caught the next elevator. Adam noticed that Stan Lansky had not returned Molly's pen.

Chapter Thirteen

"It's not even three o'clock," Molly said. "If we wanted to, we could stop by Pierce's loft downtown. I've got the keys."

"The only place we're headed is the police station." Adam ushered her into the passenger side of his car. "Our investigation is over."

"Not necessarily," she said. "I mean, we'll tell Berringer about everything, but we can—"

"Stop, Molly."

"Maybe we could—"

"What part of 'danger, danger, danger' do you not understand?"

But she didn't want to give up.

She stared through the windshield as he got behind the steering wheel and started the engine. Of course, the note was significant, but it didn't mean they had to quit. "Come on, Adam. Aren't you curious? Don't you want to take a look at Pierce's loft?"

"Not without backup."

Backup? They'd been dashing around all day without backup. Until now, Adam had seemed convinced that he could handle any threat alone. Why was he being so übercautious. "What did Pierce say to you?"

"Before I tell you, look in your purse."

She eyed him curiously. "I already had one surprise in my purse today."

"See if there's anything missing."

A weird request. She opened her oversized bag. Though she applied her organizational principles to sorting the necessary stuff she carried in her purse, it never worked very well. During the course of a regular day, everything got jumbled together. She enumerated the objects. "Cell phone. Wallet. Makeup pouch. Notepad."

She ran her hand along the bottom. "Where's my pen? That was a really nice silver pen. I hope I didn't lose it."

"You didn't," Adam said.

When had she last used the pen? She remembered giving it to Stan Lansky at the hospital. He handed the notepad back to her. But the pen? "Stan swiped my pen."

"Your shiny silver pen," Adam pointed out. "What does that suggest to you?"

"He's the magpie."

As soon as she said it, she knew it was true. Stan Lansky fit the profile for a petty thief—not bold enough for real crime, not motivated by profit but something far more sinister. Though he seemed quiet and unassuming, easy to ignore among all these other extravagant personalities who plied their trade in the wedding biz, Stan was a very angry man. As the magpie, he could strike back.

"That poor, frustrated, resentful little man." She remembered the long-suffering look in Stan's eyes when Heidi changed her mind ten times within as many minutes. "He puts up with a lot of guff."

"He sure as hell does," Adam agreed wholeheartedly. "I'm surprised he hasn't gone completely berserk."

Something about this theory didn't quite click. "But how could he be the magpie? Nobody invites the tailor to their wedding."

"Only one robbery took place at the actual wedding reception," Adam said.

"The Deitrich wedding." She glanced over her shoulder into the backseat. The brown envelope that Ronald had given her was still there. "We'll look through these candid photos. If Stan is there, I'd have to say that we've caught our thief."

"But first," Adam said as he pulled out of the parking lot and merged into traffic, "we talk to the police."

She took the cell phone from her purse and held it toward him. "You should call and make sure Berringer is there before we go to the cop shop."

"You know I don't talk on the phone while I'm driving."

"Heaven forbid."

"You call Berringer."

Her stomach turned. "I'd rather eat worms."

In a way, she hated to turn Stan over to the cops. He was a fairly sympathetic character. But she couldn't ignore the clues, and Berringer needed to be informed. Resigned to the inevitable, she speed-dialed the main number for the Denver Police department. It took only a few minutes to reach Ted Berringer, who wasn't in his office. She arranged to meet him in a few minutes at a tavern in north Denver and gave the directions to Adam.

She sank back in her seat and adjusted the seat belt across her breasts. "At least, we have one part of the puzzle figured out. Stan Lansky is the magpie."

"There's more to think about," Adam said. "How do Stan's relatively quiet crimes fit into the violence? The bloody attack on Pierce? And the attempted assault on you?"

Molly considered for a moment. "If Pierce confronted Stan about the petty theft, Stan might have attacked him."

"Let's take a critical look at that idea," Adam said. "Stan's not a tall man. He probably only comes up to Pierce's shoulder."

"And he definitely wasn't the person in black who came after me."

"He has a partner," Adam suggested.

"I don't think so. There's not enough money involved in stolen appliances and trinkets to warrant a partnership. If Stan is the magpie, he isn't working for a profit. He has his own twisted personal reasons. Resentment. Frustration. Veiled hostility."

Adam glanced over at her. "You sound like one of our volunteer psychological profilers."

"I've been paying attention to what they say."

She also had a certain expertise in spotting petty crooks. A long time ago, some were her close companions...and coworkers.

"And then, there's the note." Adam quoted, "'The crime is set.'"

"And what does that mean?" she wondered. "It sounds more important than a reference to toaster theft. What crime?"

She needed more information about Stan. As soon as Molly got to her computer at CCC, she'd check his credit and phone records. Hadn't he mentioned a wife? Where did he live? She didn't even know if he worked for Gloria full-time.

She turned back to Adam. "When you were talking to Pierce, did he say anything useful?"

"He mentioned glitter. He wasn't specific, but you and Heidi were on the same topic when he said it."

"Do you think he was talking about the glitter on her gown?"

Adam shrugged.

"That's not very helpful. Those sparkles aren't worth much. They're just glass or cubic zirconia or sequins."

"And you're the expert on sparkly things."

"Maybe he meant diamonds." She caught her breath. "The antique diamond necklace from Lucien Smythe."

That piece of fine necklace, worth eight hundred thousand, was a huge temptation for a thief—and the basis for a theory. Molly speculated, "Let's say that somebody found out about Stan and his sneaky little thievery. Now suppose that person threatened to tell."

"Blackmail," Adam said.

"And the only way they'd keep Stan's guilty secret is if he stole the necklace for them."

"Keep going."

"But Pierce found out about the planned theft and confronted Stan." Excited about how neatly this all fell into place, she gestured determinedly, pounding her fist into her hand. "That's why Pierce was attacked. So they could get away with their grand scheme to steal the necklace."

"And the attack on you?"

"They saw me as a threat. And they came after me because they were afraid I might figure it out, too."

Though Adam continued to nod encouragingly, he didn't seem totally convinced. "If I were a criminal mastermind, I wouldn't trust Stan Lansky to pull off a major heist."

He made a good point. A big-time crook would have his own experts. "Maybe the person who's putting pressure on Stan isn't usually a professional criminal."

"You're referring to someone who owns a wedding boutique. Or works as a caterer. Or a photographer."

"Gloria, Denny or Ronald," she said.

"I hope you're right," Adam said darkly. "Because I hate to think we're really in 'danger, danger, danger.'"

THE TAVERN where they met Berringer was a pleasant little neighborhood spot with leaded glass windows, dark wood tables and pizza on the menu. The detective sat alone at a center table where he was finishing off the last slice of a small pizza with pepperoni. He stood to greet them, wiping the grease from his fingers.

"Don't bother to shake hands," Molly said. She'd rather touch a spider. "Enjoy your lunch."

"You should try the pizza here. It's the best in town."

From his spreading girth, she could tell that Berringer was spending way too much time sampling pizza pies all over the greater Denver area. "No, thanks. We had pizza last night."

"Let's get down to business," Adam said. "We have information about the attack on Pierce Williams."

"Really." Berringer's tone was sour enough to curdle the milk he was drinking to wash down his pepperoni.

"I'll explain," Molly said. "When we talked before, I mentioned that several petty thefts had occurred at weddings where Pierce was the planner."

Berringer nodded as he finished wiping his fingers and discarded the paper napkin.

Cooly, she added, "Thefts that your guys didn't think merited investigation."

"I should record this interview," he said, reaching into his jacket pocket. "I sense a confession coming on."

"From me?"

"Who else?"

What a jerk! "Look, Berringer, I'm trying to do the right thing in giving you a lead. And possibly in thwarting a future crime."

"Fine. Go ahead."

In general, she wasn't somebody who got rattled. But talking to the cops made her tense. It was easy to flash back to her runaway youth. Most kids thought Mister Policeman was their friend. Her experience was different. The cops were the people who snatched her off the street and returned her to foster care.

Detective Berringer leaned his elbows on the tabletop. "I'm waiting, Molly."

"Somebody stole my pen."

There was a silence. Then Berringer said, "Still waiting."

"It's a really nice pen. Shiny and silver. It's exactly the sort of object that would attract a magpie." *Oh, swell.* Now she sounded like somebody from the Nature Channel. "What I'm trying to say is that I know who's been stealing from the weddings. I think I know."

"I don't have time for this," he said.

"They might be building up to a big heist. The petty theft was just practice."

"Hate to break it to you, Moll. But I myself have, on occasion, accidentally walked off with a pen. It's not proof." He turned to Adam. "Have you got anything resembling real evidence?"

"Hey!" She slapped the flat of her hand on the tabletop. "I'm talking here."

Molly wasn't about to lie down and let this jerk

steamroll over her ego. When it came to detecting, she'd match her research and insight against the likes of Ted Berringer any day. "This is my investigation."

"She's right," Adam said. He leaned back in his chair. "Molly's in charge."

She said, "Talk to me or talk to nobody."

"That's just great," Berringer muttered. "Do you have anything more than a pen theft? Real evidence?"

"You don't have to make an arrest," she said. "Just bring this guy in for questioning. If you put any pressure on him, he'll crack and tell you everything."

"I need a reason to pick him up. Have you got *anything?*"

Dreading what she was about to say next, Molly cringed inside. "Last night I was attacked by someone in a black ski mask. They had a knife."

"Was it the guy who stole your pen?"

She really wanted to lie and say yes, but she stuck to the truth. "I can't identify the attacker, but he or she was driving a white van."

"License plate number?"

"I didn't get one," she said.

"You should file a report on the assault," he said. "In the meantime, there's nothing I can do. No real leads. No real reason to bring anybody in for questioning."

She bit her tongue to keep from swearing. Usually, when she worked with the police through CCC, they were cooperative. "Detective Berringer, I'm not making this up. Pierce was stabbed. I was attacked. And we have reason to believe there's going to be another crime. I need your help."

"You need me?" He chuckled. "Much as I'd like to handle your needs, there's nothing I can do. I can't pick somebody up because he stole your pen. That's not going to fly."

"Then I guess this is goodbye." She pushed back her chair and stood. "I'll wait for you in the car, Adam."

She flounced out the door of the tavern. Though she would have liked the validation of a police presence, Molly wasn't too terribly upset by Berringer's refusal to help. This was, after all, her case. And she felt able to solve it…with or without police assistance.

In less than five minutes, Adam joined her.

"Sorry," she said. It was important for CCC to maintain good relations with the police department.

"Don't apologize," he said. "Berringer is a jackass."

"Did you give him the note?"

"I did. And I told him about the antique diamond necklace."

"What did he say?"

"He'll look into it. I had the distinct impression that this case is ninety-nine on a priority list of one hundred." He reached over to pat her arm. "I'm sorry Berringer gave you a hard time."

"Thanks for taking my side."

He gave her a warm smile. "I guess our investigation is back on, Molly."

"I'm glad," she said. "But are you sure this isn't going to create future problems with the police and CCC?"

"Hell, no. The reason I started CCC in the first place was to investigate crimes—past and present—that had the authorities baffled. This fits the bill."

As she smiled back at him, it dawned on her that she had something else to worry about—something other than anonymous notes, knife-wielding psychos and reluctant cops. Tonight, she'd be staying at Adam's house, sleeping alone in his guest bedroom, and Amelia wouldn't be there as a buffer.

Adam's bedroom was two doors away from the guest room. She could sleepwalk that far with her eyes closed. Was she ready to take their relationship to the next level? To make love to Adam?

In many ways, the idea appealed to her. They'd waited seven years for a kiss. If she left the timing up to him, they'd both be retirement age before anything else happened.

On the other hand, she still wasn't over her uncomfortable feelings about Adam's transformation from her mentor to a possible lover. If they made love too soon, it might ruin their friendship and working relationship. Was a kiss just a kiss? Did it mean something more? Should she go to bed with him?

"You're quiet," Adam said.

"Thinking."

"About what?"

She studied his profile. His deep-set eyes focused on the road as they headed back toward Golden. He didn't have a single hair out of place; Adam had a standing appointment with the barber every three weeks. What would it be like to run her fingers through his hair? Would he be irritated?

In her experience, lovemaking was messy and imprecise with a lot of groping. But she didn't expect Adam to be clumsy. He never left anything to chance. Before he had sex, he'd probably memorized the *Kama Sutra.*

"Well, Molly. What are you thinking about?"

She wasn't ready for this conversation. "Dinner."

FOR MOST OF HIS LIFE outside the Marine Corps, Adam had cooked for himself. He'd learned the basics as a kid, preparing dinner for his sister when his parents were preoccupied. And he hadn't gone much further down the culinary road. His taste was simple. Meat, potatoes and sometimes a salad.

Though the kitchen at his house was large, Molly took up a lot of space as she whipped open cabinet doors and peered into the fridge.

"Where are your spices?" she asked.

He pointed to a lazy Susan on the granite counter-top. "Salt. Pepper. Sugar. Crushed red pepper."

"That's it? No garlic? No cayenne? No oregano?"

"Somebody gave me a spice rack for a housewarming present," he said. "But I threw it out after a couple of years."

"I can't believe we've never cooked together," she said. "Apron?"

"Got one." He opened the pantry door and took a plain black apron from the hook.

"Put it on me," she said. "I don't want splatters on my sweater."

He looped the top of the apron over her head, being careful not to mess her hair. Then he reached behind her to tie the apron strings. They were close—so close that he could feel the warmth radiating from her body. Close enough for another kiss.

His bedroom was right up the staircase. If he kissed her now, they might never make dinner. Not that he cared about the food. His hunger was much deeper.

"Thanks," she said. Her voice was breathy. Her full lips parted seductively.

"You're more than welcome." *Welcome into my heart, my life, my bed.*

But Molly stepped away from his impromptu embrace and backed against the countertop. She swallowed so hard that he could almost hear the gulp. "I'm going to show you how to turn a totally boring flank steak into beef Stroganoff."

"That's not a lesson I'm particularly interested in."

She turned away from him to wash her hands at the sink. "Adam, I'm not sure what to do. The idea of, um, being with you. Well, it isn't like anything that's ever happened to me before."

"Why?"

"Because I already have all kinds of feelings about you." She turned to face him. "You're my boss. And you're more than that. Seven years ago, you took me under your wing. You encouraged me. Everything I am today, I owe to you."

"I'm not a saint, Molly."

"Way back then, why did you reach out to me?"

"To turn you in for picking pockets would have been a waste. You're bright. And kind. I've never known anyone so accepting. You have the people skills I lack."

The glow from her eyes gave him immense pleasure. He wanted to please her in every way.

"Also," she said, "you needed a secretary."

"I'm a practical man."

"A good man." A frown pinched her forehead, and she bit her lower lip. He had never seen her so uncertain. In a tiny voice, she said, "I don't know if I can be good enough for you."

Her words knifed into his soul. Not good enough? Clearly, she didn't know how lovely she was. She didn't realize that when she walked into a room, it became luminous.

His gaze lingered on her shining blond hair and her sweet mouth. In her eyes, he saw self-doubt that came from her childhood, her failed marriage and her brush with crime. It would take more than words to convince her that she was worthy of the finest, the best, the most astounding treasures life had to offer.

All of a sudden, he knew what should happen next. A plan leapt into his head, fully formed.

"When we make love," he said, "I want it to be perfect. For you."

Her eyes widened suspiciously. "What do you mean?"

"We'll be at Heidi's wedding this weekend. Tomorrow is Friday, and I intend to book a suite at the Brown Palace." It was the finest old hotel in Denver. And he'd do everything right. The flowers. The wine. The classy dinner from room service. "Will you join me?"

She took both his hands in hers and squeezed gently. "I will."

"It's settled."

She dropped his hands and turned back to the countertop. "Let's get cooking. Literally."

He was pleased with himself. Tomorrow night couldn't come soon enough.

Chapter Fourteen

After their Stroganoff dinner, which Adam had to admit was delicious, he cleared the dining-room table.

Molly spread out the candid photographs from the Deitrich wedding reception across the tabletop, and they sorted through them together. It was a homey exercise, like putting together a photo album. But they were using somebody else's wedding.

Though the poses were unrehearsed, most of the pictures were flattering—subtly catching a moment. Couples dancing. Two bridesmaids in matching gowns with their heads together. The best man holding up his wine glass for a toast.

Adam had to admit, "Ronald does nice work."

"I had no idea he was so talented," she said. "Maybe I should let him do those sexy pictures of me."

"Only if I can watch."

She held up a close-up photo of Pierce and Gloria, chatting with their heads together. "The way he's looking at her makes it hard to believe their marriage is over."

"Maybe the divorce wasn't his idea."

"How can he care about her?" Molly shook her head in disgust. "She's a witch. A monster. She's Medusa on a bad-hair day."

But did he love her? Was he protecting her? Adam recalled his brief conversation with Pierce in the hospital. He hadn't spoken Gloria's name, hadn't referred to her specifically. In fact, he'd said he loved Molly. "Your friend Pierce is more complex than I expected."

"How so?"

"He's obviously shielding the person who stabbed him. Ignoring the risk to himself." No matter how misguided this action, Adam had to admire Pierce's selfless sense of honor—sacrificing himself rather than betraying another. "He knows this situation is dangerous. He talked about bad people. Evil people."

"Aha," she said. "That's why you got so protective and said we needed backup. Evil people. You're thinking about professional criminals."

"Possibly." When Adam thought they were investigating boutique owners and caterers, his concern for safety was low-key. He could handle an assault from any of their current list of suspects without breaking a sweat. "We need to be prepared for serious bad guys."

She leaned back in her chair. "I'd have to say that the person who attacked me wasn't a hit man. Much as I like to think of myself as a kung fu princess, I'm not that lethal."

"I tend to agree," he said. "Your attacker used a knife. If a hit man was hired to take you out, he'd use a gun."

She winced. "I'm glad I was dealing with an amateur."

"The assault on Pierce is a different story. If you hadn't showed up when you did, Pierce would be dead."

"You think it was the work of a hit man."

"It was neatly planned. A clunk on the head. A knife in the back."

"But the blade missed his heart."

"By only a few centimeters." Adam had attended several autopsies, enough to know that the workings of the human body were complex and unpredictable. "Even a surgeon would have a hard time making a sure kill with one stab."

"If you really wanted to kill somebody, you'd slice the carotid artery."

"That might have been the intention," Adam said. "But you interrupted before the hit man could finish the job."

Molly remembered her panic on that night when she fumbled in the darkness, unsure of herself and terrified. Had she sensed the presence of evil? Had she known, deep in her bones, that the person who stabbed Pierce was a killer?

The attack in the parking lot had a completely different feel. Of course, she was scared. But she was able to fight back. "Could it have been two different attackers?"

"It's possible." Adam returned his attention to the array of photos on the table. He held one up for her to see. "Here's Stan."

"Our little magpie."

She studied the picture. Like the other men attending the wedding, Stan Lansky wore a dark suit. He was perfectly groomed and polished, looking very classy on the dance floor.

The real surprise was his dancing partner. The small, delicate blonde was a knockout. She wore a simple, elegant, floor-length gown with lace sleeves. Her hair was upswept in curls. She couldn't have been older than her midtwenties. "Is this Stan's wife?"

"From the way he's holding her, it looks like they've danced together before."

She'd imagined Stan being married to someone his

own age, in her midforties. Not necessarily a frumpy woman, but solid and housewifely—the sort who baked cookies and planned weekend activities like painting the garage or cleaning the gutters.

Molly hadn't expected the little tailor to be married to a blond bombshell. "Wow! You go, Stan."

"He'd steal for her," Adam said. "Sparkly things to keep her happy."

"Plus," Molly said. "Stan could make her fabulous clothes. It's not a bad thing to be married to a master tailor."

THE NEXT DAY, she and Adam set out with backup. They were accompanied by Tony, a retired Navy SEAL who volunteered at CCC as a bodyguard. He was a formidable presence—big, silent and strong. It was only after Molly got to know him that she realized Tony was a teddy bear.

At nine o'clock, they showed up unannounced at Gloria's boutique. The perky young thing at the front desk had a nervous look as soon as she recognized Molly. She busied her hands, rearranging her pens and straightening the white appointment book. "Gloria doesn't want to see you," she said.

"She'll change her mind," Molly said with the absolute confidence of someone who had not one but two very masculine, very intimidating bodyguards backing her up.

She breezed past the showroom full of gowns and headed toward the less glamorous rear storage area where Stan worked. As soon as she opened the door, she heard Gloria's voice. Though she wasn't shouting, every syllable dripped with venomous rage.

"It's horrible," Gloria said. "This gown wasn't designed to look like a snow princess."

"But the bride wants—"

"I don't care what that little twit wants. I have a reputation. I can't have my good name associated with this, this, this…" her voice rose on each word "…this grotesque glitter bomb of a dress."

Molly cleared her throat, and Gloria turned away from Heidi's gown, which hung from a padded hanger.

"You!" Gloria snarled.

Her eyes flamed, and Molly felt the heat. She quickly pulled Adam forward. "You remember Adam. And this is Tony."

Gloria didn't bother to acknowledge the two men. "This time, Molly, you've gone too far."

"You're referring to my advice about Heidi's gown?"

"First, Pierce tells Heidi to raise the hem and show off her ankles. I mean, really! Who looks at ankles? Then, you! A person with no design credentials. A person of questionable taste…" She paused to sneer at Molly's outfit of high-heeled black boots and leggings with a yellow miniskirt and yellow blouse under a black sweater that fit snugly over her breasts. "You look like a bumblebee on hormones."

"You'd best beware my sting." Molly had taken just about all of Gloria's ego-driven rage as she could stand.

"Where do you get off giving fashion advice?" She yanked at the sparkles on Heidi's dress. "This beautifully designed gown is all tarted up. Because of you."

"Heidi likes it," Molly said.

"She doesn't know what she likes. Brides can't think clearly for themselves. That's why they come to me for advice."

"And you don't hesitate to take advantage." Molly's temper was rising. "You pump up the costs on these supposedly one-of-a-kind gowns."

"My gowns are unique. Handsewn in Bangkok."

"Another way to hike up the price," Molly accused. "You probably use the services of a sweatshop, then quadruple the charges to the bride."

"What the hell do you know about my business?"

Gloria jabbed a finger in Molly's direction, and her two bodyguards stepped forward. Not that Molly needed their help. She could handle Gloria.

When she first met this woman, Molly had been intimidated, even a bit embarrassed by the boutique owner's overwhelming chic and confidence. But not anymore.

"Gloria, your business isn't all that complicated. You're a shopkeeper. Nothing more."

She bristled. "My reputation is—"

"Don't care," Molly said. "It doesn't matter how many designer outfits you've got hanging in your closet. You'll never have real style because that comes from inside. You're too angry. And you're too mean."

Gloria's mouth gaped like a trout out of water.

Molly continued, "Your job is to make your customers happy. With Heidi, you failed. That's why she turned to Pierce. And to me."

"I want you and your two thugs out of here. Right now."

"Actually, I didn't come to see you. I want to talk to Stan."

"Get out. Or I'll—"

"What?" Molly got up in her face. "What are you going to do? Stab me?"

Though she hadn't directly accused Gloria of attacking Pierce, the implication was clear. And Gloria reacted with a gasp. "How dare you!"

"You might be surprised by what I'd dare. The only reason I'm here is to help Pierce. I'm going to be handling the wedding planner details this weekend. If that means making Heidi happy with a few more sparkles on her gown, so be it."

Without another word, Gloria pivoted on her heel and stormed toward the rear of the store room. The door slammed loudly behind her.

"Well," Molly said, "Elvis has left the building."

Behind her back, she heard Tony chuckle.

She turned to him and winked, then pulled up a smile for Stan Lansky. Even if he was the magpie, the little tailor was one of the more pleasant people involved in this affair. She went toward him and patted his shoulder. "These alterations are beautiful," she said. "Heidi wanted a snowflake look, and you've caught it."

"Thank you," he choked out.

Wanting to put him at ease, she settled onto a stool beside Stan and posed a nonthreatening question. "These gowns are made in Bangkok. How does that work?"

"Not all of the gowns come from Thailand," he said.

"Which ones are imported?"

"It depends on the designer and the complexity of the gown, especially those that require detailed beading." He warmed to the topic. "It'd be a waste of time and money to ship a plain sheath halfway around the world."

"I understand," she said. "Which designers do you use?"

"All the big names, including Armani and Vera Wang. And, of course, Gloria does her own designs. All of her dresses come through Bangkok."

"Like Heidi's dress?"

Ruefully, he nodded. "That's why she's so upset."

Too bad! Molly would spare no sympathy for Gloria.

When Adam stepped forward to join them, she

wished she could warn him that this wasn't the right time for a good cop/bad cop scene. Stan was already quaking. More hostility might turn him into a mass of Jell-O.

But Adam seemed to instinctively understand her concerns. Cordially, he said, "This is a complex process. How do you do it?"

"It's not hard. I take the bride's measurements, and Gloria coordinates with the designers and the seamstress to make sure the fabrics are precisely correct. Then, the gowns are shipped here."

"But they still require alterations," Adam said.

As Stan's head bobbed, the glare from the overhead light flickered off his balding head. "Or else I wouldn't have a full-time job."

"You work fast," Molly said. "You managed to put all these shimmers on Heidi's dress overnight."

Stan beckoned them closer and whispered, "Sometimes, I've made the whole gown. And the bridesmaid's dresses."

"That must be satisfying," Adam said.

But Molly had concerns about the ethics of this arrangement. "You're not sewing designer knockoffs, are you?"

"Certainly not." He was honestly affronted. "The dresses I've made are original designs from Gloria."

Still looking for the criminal side, Molly visualized the start of a sweatshop right here in Denver. And Stan Lansky was the number one employee. "I hope Gloria pays you extra."

"She's a generous employer," he said, staunchly defending her. "Alterations don't take up all of my time. Someday, Gloria might let me do my own original designs."

"I bet you'd be good at it," she said soothingly. "Maybe you already do some of your own designing. For your friends. Or your wife."

A tiny smile quirked his mouth. "My wife says we should start our own bridal boutique. She could be my model. She's not tall enough for couture, but she's very pretty. Much more pretty than most of these rich brides."

Molly detected a chord of hostility, and she played on it. "I meant what I said to Gloria. Style doesn't come from money. You can't buy class."

Stan nodded. "My wife has class. She's sweet and innocent and she deserves the best of everything."

"Do you have a photo?"

Stan pulled out his wallet and flipped it open. On one side was his driver's license. On the other was a glamour shot of the young blonde who he'd been dancing with at the Deitrich wedding reception.

Both Adam and Tony came forward to look. Both made appropriately admiring comments.

"You're right," Molly said. "She deserves the very best."

"Sometimes," he said, "I get so angry when these brides throw money around like it's nothing. What did they ever do to merit such finery?"

"Like Heidi?"

"I don't mind her." He shrugged. "At least she pays attention to me. Most of these women don't even bother to learn my name."

"They'll be sorry when you're a famous designer."

"That's right."

With a final, longing glance at his wife's photo, he closed his wallet. Then he went to his suit coat that was hanging on a rack beside several gowns in dry cleaner bags. He reached into the inner pocket. "After I got home last night, I realized that I accidentally took your pen, Molly."

As he held out the silver pen to her, Molly's suspicions crumbled. She liked Stan Lansky. Maybe he wasn't the magpie, after all.

"IT's GOT TO be him," Adam said as he parked on the street in the trendy area known as LoDo for Lower Downtown Denver. Pierce's loft was nearby. "I don't know why Stan gave your pen back, but he's the magpie."

"I'm not so sure," Molly said.

"It's him."

Adam wouldn't let go of the one conclusion they'd managed to draw. Stan Lansky was the magpie. He fit the bill: motive, method and opportunity.

He had the opportunity to commit these petty crimes because he was acquainted with the wedding schedules and possibly had visited the homes of the brides for final fittings of their gowns.

Regarding method, the thefts varied in the ways they were committed. In Stan's profession as a tailor, he was clever with his hands.

But the most damning evidence in Adam's mind was evidence that could not be specifically quantified: motive. When Stan talked about these wealthy brides, his resentment was blatant. Stan felt as if he deserved more, deserved all the lavish wedding gifts. Which he would then present as prizes to his attractive young wife. Oh yeah, Stan Lansky was the magpie.

After plugging all his spare change into the parking meter, Adam walked beside Molly on the sidewalk. Tony brought up the rear. Though it had been a waste of time to drag Tony along to the boutique, it was good to have backup. Adam didn't know what to expect inside the loft that Pierce had told him was leased.

Last night, Molly had researched that statement by studying the personal financial statements they'd taken from Pierce's town house. Every month, Pierce received a substantial check from the Sylvan Company for rent on this address.

But Gloria and Denny had been interested enough in this property to remove the file from Pierce's personal files. Their actions were suspicious enough to merit this further investigation.

Molly glanced up at him. "Did you have time to take care of that other thing?"

"What other thing?"

She whispered, "The room at the Brown Palace?"

"A suite," he said. "It's booked."

He'd enjoyed making the arrangements himself. Usually, the reservation of hotel rooms or rental cars was a task he assigned to Molly. Handling it himself emphasized that tonight was different. Tonight was special. "Everything will be taken care of. All you need to bring is yourself."

"Okay." She turned to pull Tony into their conversation. "What do you think about all the wedding stuff?"

"Been there, done that."

Adam grinned at Tony's stoic comment, spoken like a man who had been married for thirty-five years.

Molly said, "When you got married, I'll bet your wife did all the planning."

"Still does," he said. "I just go where I'm told and try to stay out of trouble."

"Wise man," Adam said.

"Honestly," Molly said, "you guys make it sound like women are the adversary."

"Hell, no. I've already surrendered," Tony said. "She's the boss."

"And if you step out of line, what happens?"

This big, tough, former Navy SEAL cringed. "We have a relationship talk."

"A fate worse than death," Molly said dryly.

Adam didn't think he'd mind talking about relationships with Molly. Because they'd known each other for so long, he figured there shouldn't be many surprises.

In the lobby of the converted brick building where Pierce had a loft on the eighth floor, he turned to Tony. "I'm not sure what to expect in here. Be ready for a confrontation."

"Right."

As Molly found the right key and opened the outer door to the lobby, he said to her, "You stay down here. Tony and I will secure the premises and I'll call you on the cell phone when we're sure it's safe."

"You want me to stay out here on the street?" Her eyebrows raised. "Is it safe for me to be here by myself?"

He frowned. Her logic was correct. If somebody was after her, she'd be an easy target on the street. "Maybe we should walk you back to the car."

"Where a white van could pull up beside me?" She shook her head. "The point of having you be my bodyguard is…for you to guard my body."

Tony chuckled. "She's got you there, pal."

"I'm coming with you," Molly said breezily. "No arguments, Adam. I have the keys."

No surprises. Her attitude had always been sassy and feisty. She could be a regular pain in the rear.

And tonight? He might see a different side of Molly.

Chapter Fifteen

Riding in the elevator to the eighth floor, Molly subtly inched back until she was almost touching Adam's chest. He rested his hand lightly on her hip, and their slight physical contact excited her. Later today, that contact would deepen. They'd share the night at the Brown Palace Hotel, and she wished she could concentrate only on that event.

Unfortunately, she couldn't escape the tension that came along with this investigation. Adam and Tony were her bodyguards, and there was a reason for them to watch over her. DANGER. DANGER. DANGER.

If something bad happened to her or to Adam before tonight, she'd know for sure that her life was cursed, and she just wasn't destined to be happy. Not now. Not ever. The closer she came to a real loving relationship, the less she dared to believe it was going to happen. She'd never been lucky.

Outside the elevator on the eighth floor, she eyed the long hallway. Refinished wood baseboards and old-fashioned wall sconces maintained the historic atmosphere in this building. If she recalled correctly, this place had once been a bank, and there was an old, walk-in safe in the basement. "It's so quiet in here."

"Solid brick walls," Adam said. "They built them to last in the old days."

"It's hard to believe mobs of people are just outside the front door." She liked the sense of isolation, finding a quiet nest in the middle of a bustling metropolis. "I wouldn't mind living here."

"Not me," Adam said. "I don't care for city living. When I walk out the door, I want to see grass and trees, not sidewalks."

Outside the loft apartment, Adam and Tony drew their sidearms. Their readiness increased her foreboding. *If anything happened to her...or to Adam...*

No matter how much she wanted to deny the danger, it was ever-present and increasing. Someone had tried to murder Pierce. Someone had attacked her. She wasn't visiting this loft for a party this time.

Adam knocked on the door and waited for a response. He knocked again.

Silence. The narrow hallway was utterly still. The air hung heavy and cool. Molly shivered, wondering if ghosts from the Old West inhabited these walls. Maybe she didn't want to live here, after all.

Adam held out his hand. "Key."

She closed her fingers around the key ring. "What are you going to do?"

"Tony and I will secure the premises."

"Does that mean you're going to charge through the rooms, waving your guns?"

"Essentially."

"You can't do that," she said. "According to Pierce's records, somebody lives here. They might be completely innocent."

"We're not taking that chance," Adam said.

Though she agreed with him in theory, she felt uncomfortable about the SWAT-team approach. If Adam and Tony charged inside unannounced, any rational person would freak out. Any litigious person would call their attorney.

"I need the key," Adam repeated.

With a scowl, she handed him the key ring. "What should I do?"

"Much as I'd like to have you out of harm's way, stay with me."

With a nod to Tony, Adam pushed the door open. As she followed, he and Tony made their way through the spacious loft, checking in closets and opening all doors. Nobody was home.

Molly returned to the front room to close and lock the door. Breathing more easily, she approached the three large arched windows that rose from the floor to eight feet high. Two other tall buildings interfered with a panorama of the front range, but it was still a magnificent view of snow-capped peaks. Ski season would be under way in only a month.

"Nobody lives here," Adam said. "The closets are empty."

But the loft was fully furnished. The leather upholstered furniture was attractive and definitely expensive though not very imaginative. "It reminds me of a hotel suite."

"No personal knickknacks on the shelves," Adam noted. "Not like the place Pierce lives where he's got a bunch of athletic trophies."

Molly wandered aimlessly, unsure of what she should be looking for. She paused at a wall display of black-and-white photographs. "Nice artwork."

Adam stepped up beside her. "Too modern for my taste."

A frustrated sigh pursed her lips. She and Adam were so completely different. She liked the city; he liked grassy yards. She preferred modern art. These photos were close-ups of body parts.

"It's not abstract," she said. "Look. There's a belly button. And this has got to be one naked thigh on top of another. Two people. I think we know what they're doing."

"Sex," Adam said bluntly. "It's cold. Too detached."

She lifted an eyebrow. "What kind of nudes do you like?"

"The ones I can touch."

"That's not very artsy."

He smiled. "Wait and see."

Molly felt herself beginning to blush. Looking for a distraction, she checked the signature on the photos. "Ronald Atchison."

"I wonder how else he's connected to this loft."

She reached into her purse and pulled out her cell phone. "I could call him and find out."

"Do you think he'd say anything?"

"Maybe," she said. "I think you shook him up yesterday. Now, he's had time to think. He might want to come clean."

"About what?" Adam asked.

"Yesterday, when you were in Ronald's face being the bad cop, you mentioned fake IDs. And I think he reacted to that."

Adam nodded. "But how do fake IDs fit in with the theft of the diamond necklace?"

"Not very well."

Tony called out from the kitchen, "Come in here and check out the fridge."

Like the rest of the spacious loft, the kitchen looked

expensive with a top-of-the-line oven and a double-door, stainless steel refrigerator. Tony stood beside the fridge, holding the door open and pointing inside.

Molly grinned at him. "You look posed. Like one of those models who show off appliances."

"Only not so pretty," Adam said.

Molly looked where Tony was pointing. "I see mustard, horseradish and bottled water. There's got to be twenty bottles in there, and it's the same brand Denny Devlin served us."

Tony swung open the freezer section. Inside were several prepackaged meals, ready for the microwave. But these weren't the usual meals Molly purchased at the supermarket. The containers were plain white with the contents handwritten on the side. She took one out and read the logo printed across the top: Devlin Catering.

"That ties two of our primary suspects to this place," Adam said.

"There might be an innocent explanation," she said. "Maybe Pierce rents this place as a kind of corporate suite for visiting executives. Of course, he'd use the people he knows to provide services. Like Denny for the food. Ronald for the artwork. If we knew more about the other people associated with weddings, we'd likely find connections to them as well."

"Where do the rent checks come from?" Adam asked.

"The Sylvan Company." She'd never heard of this corporation. "When I tried to check out the company, I found nothing but a checking account."

"Who signs the checks?"

"Nobody connected with the wedding business," she said. "I can dig deeper into ownership, but it will take a while if this isn't a Colorado corporation."

"We might not have the time," Adam said.

Tony nodded. "Not if the criminals are after that diamond necklace. The wedding's tomorrow."

"Tony, I'm so glad you're going to be there," Molly said. "What happened when you met with Lucien Smythe?"

"We worked out details for transport of the necklace." Tony shrugged. "He's a solid citizen. Former Navy."

But Molly knew that Lucien was far from your typical citizen. Not only did he have a criminal record, but he'd taken it upon himself to hack off the finger of a thief.

She frowned. The more they learned, the more suspicious everyone looked. And, somehow, it always came back around to Pierce.

She took out her cell phone, intending to call him. When she activated her phone, she found the message box full. "People have been trying to reach me."

She scrolled through the list. "Denny called. And a florist. The cake baker. Heidi called five times." Obviously, Molly needed to pay more attention to the last-minute details for the wedding tomorrow. "There's even a call from Pierce in the hospital."

And that was the number she needed to contact first. With a few quick questions to Pierce, she might be able to understand the real purpose of this loft.

He picked up immediately, and she was pleased to hear him sounding healthy and strong.

"Molly, I have to ask a favor."

"Shoot."

"I want you to step out of Heidi's wedding plans. Gloria will take over from here."

Though Molly had no professional stake in this business and had done very little to keep Heidi's wedding on track, she was insulted. "Are you firing me?"

"Don't take it that way," he said. "I just don't want you in the middle of this. Adam told me that somebody attacked you."

"I handled it." And she could handle the wedding, too. All it took was a couple of phone calls.

"Please," he said. "Back off."

She sensed that there was something more involved in Pierce's decision. "Did Gloria ask you to get me out of the picture?"

"It's possible."

"She's standing right there, isn't she? She's in your hospital room."

"That's right."

It figured. Gloria had gone directly from their confrontation at her boutique to the hospital. At this very moment, that witch was circling Pierce's bed on her broomstick. "I'm sorry she bothered you. You should be concentrating on getting better. Not worrying about weddings."

"It's my job," he said. "So, we're agreed."

"Not entirely." Molly had made necessary arrangements that she didn't want Gloria to interfere with. "The additional security on Lucien Smythe's necklace is not to be changed."

"Additional security?" Pierce questioned. "Why?"

Good grief! Had it escaped his notice that there was a knife-wielding psycho on the loose? "The necklace is worth over eight hundred thousand dollars. Extra security can't hurt."

"Sure," he said amiably. "Fine."

"And Adam and I will attend the wedding reception."

There was a pause. "I'd rather you didn't."

"Listen, Pierce, you were the one who asked me to look into your petty thefts." Though her totally justifiable anger was building, she kept her voice calm. It wasn't her intention to hassle him in the hospital. "Whether I like it or not, I'm involved. And I need answers before some hit man decides to take me out of the picture."

"Nothing is going to happen at Heidi's wedding," he said.

But she wasn't so sure. The anonymous note said that the crime would take place on Saturday at the same time as Heidi's wedding and reception. It couldn't be a coincidence. "We won't go to the ceremony, but Adam and I intend to stake out the reception."

"Just stay safe," he said. "Stay out of trouble."

"Little old me? When have I ever gotten in trouble?"

"Not funny," he said. "Anything else?"

Standing at the window in his loft, she remembered the reason for this phone call. "Your loft in LoDo. Tell me about the person who rents it."

"I only met him once. His credit checked out. He's an entrepreneur who moved to Denver from someplace back east."

"What's his business?"

"The Sylvan Company," Pierce said. "That's how he pays the rent."

"Did you rent the loft furnished?"

"No way. I'm not a decorator." He paused. "Adam asked me about the loft, too. What's going on?"

"Nothing you need to worry about. Get well, Pierce."

She disconnected the call and stood quietly for a moment, gazing out at the Rockies, and wondering about the connections in this loft. If Pierce hadn't furnished the place, why were Ronald Atchison's artsy photos decorating the walls? Why would Denny Devlin have provided microwave food?

The missing link had to be Gloria. She'd swiped the file from Pierce's home office, hoping to keep Molly from learning more about the Sylvan Company and the mysterious entrepreneur who rented this classy loft.

Somehow, Molly knew, this place was central to the crime. Whatever that crime might be.

AFTER A BIT of catch-up work at the CCC offices, Molly was escorted to her house by Tony, the bodyguard. She needed to pack some clothes for the wedding reception tomorrow and something to wear tonight. At the Brown Palace. In a suite. With Adam.

Yikes! There was less than an hour left before their late afternoon check-in. The butterflies in her stomach had formed a chorus line and were high-kicking like the Rockettes.

In her bedroom, she scanned her selection of lingerie. Since Molly was unable to resist pretty underthings and sleepwear, there were plenty of choices. A slinky black chemise with feathers. A sweet pink gown that skimmed her curves.

She rejected the lacy white peignoir. It was too bride-ish, and she didn't want Adam to freak out. He was so uncomfortable around girly things. Maybe she should forget the fancy nightware altogether. But this night was supposed to be perfect for her, and she wanted to feel gorgeous.

She grabbed her cell phone and called Ronald, who answered quickly.

"Well, Molly," he said coldly, "I see you've been booted from the wedding planner business in favor of Gloria."

Ignoring his sneer, she said, "If you wanted to be really gorgeous and sexy would you wear black lingerie or pink?"

"It depends on who's going to see it. Your fiancé?"

She had almost forgotten about her fake engagement. "Right. The fiancé."

"Tell me about the black," he said.

"It's short and has feathers."

"Perfect. Wear it with a black garter belt."

"Yeah, sure. And maybe I should carry a whip. And I think we've got some handcuffs at the office."

"Sweetie, that's the spirit."

Why on earth had she expected to get decent fashion advice from Ronald? "I saw some of your photo work today. At Pierce's loft."

There was silence on the other end of the phone. Molly waited, but Ronald was not forthcoming. Gently, she asked, "Is there something you need to tell me about? Something about the loft?"

"Maybe I've done some favors for friends. It all seemed harmless at the time."

"What kind of favors?"

"If I tell you," he said, "will you promise not to tell your friend, Adam?"

She couldn't make that promise. "No." But she wanted the information "Yes."

"I don't believe you. This is goodbye until later, Miss Molly."

She stared at the disconnected cell phone, wishing that somebody—anybody—would break down and tell her the truth. There was a conspiracy of silence among these wedding people.

Tossing the cell phone on the bed, she returned to her study of lingerie.

Holding both the pink and the black, she went into the kitchen of her cozy two-bedroom house where Tony was sitting at the table, drinking a soda. She waved the pink, then the black. "Which one?"

He swallowed hard. "Are those dresses for a wedding?"

"For tonight." It might be a mistake to share her plans for tonight with Tony, but she didn't have any other confidant handy. "I'm staying at the Brown."

"With Adam?"

It was her turn to gulp. "Yes."

"About damn time," he said in a low rumble.

"What's that supposed to mean?"

"Ever since I started volunteering at CCC, you and Adam have acted like an old married couple. With none of the benefits."

She sank down at the table opposite him. "Is this weird that I'm talking to you about this?"

"I'm a good listener," he said. "And I have a daughter."

"She's fifteen," Molly said. "This is hardly the same thing."

"Sure it is."

"Oh? And if your daughter told you that she was planning to spend the night with a man, what would your reaction be?"

"Before or after I broke both his legs?"

"That's what I thought."

But Molly had always been comfortable around men. Her best friends, like Pierce, were men. Why shouldn't she be able to talk with a former Navy SEAL who was capable of leg-breaking? "I'm kind of scared about tonight."

"You? Scared?"

"Right now, Adam is probably the most important person in my life. What if being, um, intimate with him messes up our working relationship? What if he doesn't like me?"

"Not possible," Tony said with a kind smile.

"Of course it's possible. So many things can go wrong. I could blurt out something that turns him off. Maybe he won't like the way I look." She usually wasn't bothered in the least with self-esteem issues in that department. She liked her appearance. "What if Adam doesn't think I'm…you know…pretty."

"He does," Tony said. "All day today, he's been staring at you and drooling like a dog who wants a bone."

"Charming comparison," she said.

"Hell, you and Adam have already done the hard part of a relationship. You know you can get along on a day-to-day basis."

That was true. She and Adam teased. They disagreed on practically everything, but they accepted their differences. "Sex changes things."

"For the better," Tony said. "I couldn't be more pleased that you two have finally figured out that you belong together in more ways than CCC. You're a match. And it doesn't matter what you wear."

Still, she held up the selection of lingerie again. "Which one?"

"Sexy black," he said. "And you're going to be just fine tonight."

Chapter Sixteen

Though Adam was a man who preferred to keep things plain and simple, he was enthusiastic about his plans for a romantic evening at the Brown Palace with Molly. He'd even given his strategy a title—Operation Cupid's Arrow.

He ordered three dozen long-stemmed red roses for the suite and half a dozen candles. A Brown Palace concierge agreed, for a substantial tip, to arrange everything. Online, he checked the room service menu and preordered champagne and her favorite dinner, even though he hated asparagus.

Timing, he thought, was vital to any successful mission.

After they arrived at the suite, he'd suggest that she take a nice, relaxing bath, which was a good way to get her out of the way for the staging of his final advances. As a bonus, she'd be naked.

Then, the concierge would bring on the flowers, candlelight and dinner. When Molly came out of the tub, she'd be awed by his thoughtfulness. And she'd know how special and lovely she was.

Grinning to himself, he packed. Hopefully, he'd thought of everything.

But wait a minute! Here was a snag. What should he be wearing when she emerged from her bath? It seemed sleazy to be hanging around in his dark blue terry-cloth bathrobe. Regular khaki trousers didn't make a statement.

His tuxedo. He needed to bring the penguin suit anyway for the wedding reception tomorrow. He'd wear his tux to sweep Molly off her feet. Every woman liked a man in a tux. It was nearly as classic as his Marine dress-blue uniform.

Oh, yeah. He had this plan nailed.

When he picked Molly up at her house and loaded her suitcase into the trunk, he ran over the details in his head. What about music? Adam wasn't up on the current tunes, but he was sure the hotel had a sound system. Jazz? Classical?

"Nervous?" Molly asked.

"Not a bit." He was prepped and ready. Locked and loaded. "You?"

"This feels like a first date. But that's crazy. We've known each other forever."

"Not like this," he said.

As he drove toward Denver, the sunset glinted off the downtown skyline. The city seemed to glisten, welcoming them.

At the Brown Palace, he turned over his car to the valet and their luggage to the bellman. He took Molly's arm to escort her into the grand old hotel. The lobby was luxurious and impressive with a sweeping staircase, dangling chandelier and manteled fireplaces. A fine place for a fine lady.

Molly balked.

"What's wrong?" he asked.

"I don't belong here," she said. "Maybe we should go someplace else."

After all his careful plans? The roses and champagne? Firmly, he said, "We're staying here."

"But I'm more of a motel kind of girl. Maybe a nice motel with a swimming pool."

She'd picked a hell of a time to bare her insecurities. Usually, Molly charged into any situation whether or not she fit in. Consequences be damned.

"You deserve the Palace," he said. "And we need to be here anyway. For the wedding tomorrow."

She looked up at him doubtfully. "It does seem practical."

"Absolutely."

In their suite, her attitude improved as she checked out the solid, antique-looking furniture and the well-stocked bar. "We shouldn't drink anything from here," she said. "It'll cost a fortune."

"I've ordered a dinner," he said. Time for the next phase of his plan. "Why don't you relax? I could draw you a nice bath."

"I can run my own water," she said. "And I already took a shower at my house."

"To relax," he repeated.

"I'm fine." She flung herself onto the sofa, kicked off her high-heeled shoes and stretched out her long legs on the cushions. "Here's me. Relaxing."

Adam fiddled with the sound system. Classic rock 'n' roll blasted through the room. "I Can't Get No Satisfaction" by the Rolling Stones.

This was definitely not the mood he was going for.

Molly sang along. Boisterously.

Flipping through channels, he found a quieter station with Tony Bennett singing about leaving his heart in San Francisco.

"Leave it there," she said.

"You like the oldies."

She grinned. "I like you, don't I?"

"I'm not that old."

"I seem to recall a fortieth birthday party with black balloons and enough candles on the cake to start a forest fire. Doesn't that mean you're officially over the hill?"

"Life begins at forty."

She regarded him pensively. "How old do you think Gloria is?"

He shrugged. "I'm not good at guessing ages."

"I'd say she's closer to the big four-oh than thirty. A dangerous time of life for a woman."

"How so?"

"She starts thinking about how she's going to manage in her elder years. How she's going to pay the bills. Might be a time when a woman like Gloria could be tempted by a get-rich-quick scheme."

Operation Cupid's Arrow was floundering badly. Adam hadn't wanted to get sidetracked by talk about their investigation. Tonight should focus on them. He suggested, "Gloria's age might be a good thing for you to think about in the bathtub."

"What is it with you and the bath? I know I don't stink because I put on perfume."

He'd noticed her scent. Unlike a lot of women, Molly didn't stick with one special fragrance. Right now, she smelled like cookies—something vanilla.

She rose from the sofa and went to the complimentary fruit basket where she grabbed an apple. "Gloria is at the center of this. She's like a big, nasty spider in the middle of her web."

With a resigned sigh, Adam sank into one of the chairs beside the sofa. Operation Cupid's Arrow had been strategized for everything…except Molly. He should have known she'd be obstinate. The only way he'd get her into the tub is if he threw her over his shoulder and carried her in there. Somehow, that seemed to lack romantic finesse.

"I don't want to talk shop," he said. "All we can do now is wait. The note said the crime would take place tomorrow."

"One thing we haven't considered," she said, "is the identity of the person who wrote the anonymous note." She paused for half a second. "I think it was Ronald."

"Why?"

"I talked to him on the phone this afternoon, and he had something to confess, but he was afraid to tell me."

"I could put more pressure on him."

"No way. He'll clam up if you push. He doesn't want to go back to jail."

Right now, Adam didn't care about Ronald or the investigation. "Let's drop it. There's nothing we can do. We don't even know what the crime is."

"Obviously, it's a plan to steal the antique diamond necklace from Heidi's wedding," Molly said. "When Pierce was talking to you, he said this was about glitter. To me, that means diamonds."

"It's not so obvious," Adam said with a resigned sigh. He had considered a variety of possible crimes. Maybe if he got through them, Molly would drop this conversation and get back to the real purpose of this evening. "Forget the glitter and concentrate on Ronald. He could be selling fake IDs. Could be blackmailing someone with his wedding photos."

"Oooh." Her mouth formed a pretty O. "I like blackmail."

"As we've considered before, it could be Stan Lansky," Adam said. "Pierce figured out that he was the magpie, and Stan lashed out to save himself. And now, he's going after the necklace."

"Could be," she said. "And Denny Devlin has money troubles that could lead to criminal activity."

"Therefore," Adam said, "we can't eliminate any of our suspects."

"It all hinges on Pierce's loft," she said. "Something is going on there, and we haven't figured out the clues."

Earlier today, at the CCC offices, Molly had tried to track down details on the company that rented the loft—the Sylvan Company. There was no paper trail. The checking account had only one signatory—a guy she'd never heard of. "I still think it's Gloria. She rushed to Pierce's bedside so she could run Heidi's wedding tomorrow. Why is that so important?"

"Don't know."

She watched as Adam grabbed his suitcase and went into the bedroom, presumably to unpack. Thus far, she'd purposely avoided the bed. Though they'd come here for a romantic evening, she wasn't in the mood. There needed to be candlelight or something.

Over the radio, Tony Bennett was singing "My Way," a song that always reminded her of Adam. He did things *his* way. That was for sure. When he first started Colorado Crime Consultants, most people in law enforcement considered him to be a nuisance. They didn't think they needed advice from outside experts. The cops had been proven wrong. Time and again, CCC volunteers uncovered vital clues to solving cases.

And people loved to volunteer. From Liam MacKenzie, who used his freelance piloting business for aerial surveillance, to David Crawford, the reporter whose knowledge of serial murder was encyclopedic, the CCC volunteers were happy to share their expertise.

When Adam emerged from the bedroom, she said, "Isn't there a CCC expert we could contact for answers on this case? Somebody who would provide the final clue?"

"Pierce would be our expert on all things wedding," he said. "And he's not talking."

"Wedding details are central," she agreed. "The murder weapon was a gourmet knife a caterer would use. The tailor, Stan Lansky, is probably the magpie thief. And there's your idea about Ronald and blackmail photos."

"But who is he blackmailing?"

An idea struck her. "Somebody who's very mysterious. The guy who rents Pierce's loft and hides behind the Sylvan Company."

Adam paused for a moment, then he nodded. "Good deduction, Molly. What's his name, again?"

"Phil Prath." It was an odd name without obvious ethnic origin, and she presumed it had been shortened from something else. Another disguise. "If we find out who he really is, we'll have our answers."

Adam came toward her. His gait was slow and careful as though he was stalking her. His approach made her a little nervous.

"You're good at this," he said smoothly. "Figuring out the details."

"I like details."

He stood only a few paces away from her. Her brain was on amber alert, telling her to run and hide. But she'd agreed to this night at the Brown Palace.

Earlier, Adam's kisses had convinced her that there might be something more than friendship between them, and she was ready to explore the possibility. She'd packed her sexy black negligee.

"You're smart," Adam said.

"I should be. We've been doing this long enough, bouncing clues back and forth. It's what makes us good partners."

"I'm glad you think of us as partners," he said. "When you first started this field investigation, I wondered if you wanted to establish your own private investigation firm."

"I could," she said. "My contacts are excellent and I—"

"You'd never leave me."

"Don't be so sure." She was half teasing and half serious. "I could set up my own private eye agency."

"But you won't," he said.

"Why not? Don't you think I could handle it?"

"It's the other way around." He came one step closer. The gap between them narrowed. "Molly, I can't handle being without you."

His nearness took her breath away. "Really?"

"If you weren't there in the office, I wouldn't bother showing up. I'd be sitting alone in the dark. You're the light in my life, Molly. The sweetness in my coffee. The warmth on a winter day."

She was melting. Her insecurities washed away. "Really?"

"I need you."

She stepped into his waiting embrace, and his arms closed around her. Her nervousness vanished, and she felt very, very safe. She belonged here, after all.

When he kissed her, all thought faded from her mind. She was pure sensation. Pure excitement. Her spirit soared. She was weightless, flying. His passion—his need for her—carried her higher and higher until oxygen ran thin and she thought she might pass out from sheer euphoria.

Gasping, she ended their kiss but didn't move away from him. Now was the time. She was ready to take this attraction to the next level. She wanted to make love. "I brought a sexy black nightie."

"Not necessary," he growled.

"But I want to be extra pretty for you."

Adam smiled and kissed her forehead. "I thought I needed a romantic strategy." He kissed the tip of her nose. "Flowers and candles and champagne."

"And?" She tilted her lips up, greedy for another kiss.

"All I need is you."

He kissed her again—so deeply and thoroughly that her knees were weak. Resistance was no longer an option. She would never say no.

Gently, he scooped her off her feet and carried her into the adjoining bedroom where he placed her on the king-size bed. Slowly, he unbuttoned her blouse, trailing light kisses on each inch of newly revealed flesh.

When her blouse was completely opened, he sat on the bed, gazing down at her.

"What?" she said. Was something wrong?

"You're just so damn beautiful." He traced the line of her jaw with his thumb. "This is a perfect face."

His caress slipped down her throat to her breasts.

Molly had never been one to lie passively. She was anxious for more. More touching. More of him.

She rose up on the bed. It was her turn to touch his body. She wanted him undressed. Now.

Though she started with his buttons, her need overcame common sense. Grabbing handfuls of fabric, she ripped his shirt open, tearing the buttons apart. Her fingers stroked his naked chest. She nuzzled the springy black hair. As far as she was concerned, Adam was the truly gorgeous person in this room. His body was strong and well-proportioned.

In a burst of energy and raw need, they tore off their clothing, ripped apart the bed and collapsed together on the soft sheets.

"Slower," Adam said.

Her hand slid down his torso, and she grasped his hard erection. "You're ready."

"I want this to be good for you." His voice was husky with desire. "It takes a woman longer."

But she was already tingling all over. "Adam, I've been waiting for seven years. That's long enough."

He didn't need further encouragement. His subtle caresses became insistent. His kisses set fire to her wanton lust. She was greedy, voracious, demanding, caught up in an overwhelming passion.

Adam, always in control, sheathed himself with a condom, and when he entered her with a thrust, she thought she might explode. He drove harder and harder. Waves of pleasure rocked her body. *Yes!* This was better than she'd ever imagined. *Yes, yes, yes!*

Suspended in a state of pure ecstasy, she felt as if she were floating six feet off the mattress. And then, like a feather on the wind, she settled back down to earth. Her eyelids opened, and she gazed over at the incredible man who lay beside her.

"Adam," she whispered.

"Yes, Molly."

Mere words were incapable of expressing her fulfillment. She took his hand and kissed his knuckles.

Without warning, he snatched his hand back. He was

out of the bed. Adam stood at the door to the bedroom. Naked. Gun in hand. He stepped into the doorway and aimed with both arms straight out.

Just as quickly, he darted back. Before he closed the door, he called out, "Carry on."

"What's happening?"

"Room service," he said as he slipped back under the covers beside her. "I ordered a few things."

"When? You haven't been on the phone."

With a rueful smile, he said, "Operation Cupid's Arrow."

"And what does that mean?" She lightly ruffled the hair on his chest. "I'm really hoping that Cupid's Arrow isn't your special name for your—"

"No way."

"Explain, Adam."

"I wanted everything to be perfect for you. So I called ahead and made arrangements for food and flowers and stuff. That's why I wanted you in the bathtub—out of the way while final preparations were put into place."

"That's crazy," she said. "And so very sweet."

"I didn't count on you being such an obstinate mule, refusing to get into the bath."

"Don't apologize," she murmured. "Everything worked out for the best."

He grinned. "I'll need to tip that concierge extra. I might have startled her when I jumped into the doorway waving a gun."

"Waving a gun *and* naked," Molly said.

"Not good form," he muttered.

"Honey, there's nothing wrong with your form. But I would recommend a really huge tip." Her hand glided down his torso again. "Speaking of which—"

He caught her hand. "Not yet. I went to a lot of trouble to be romantic, and you need to see it."

She left the bed and dressed, belatedly, in her sexy black negligee.

Adam slipped into his Army-green briefs. "I was going to be wearing my tuxedo. No woman can resist a tuxedo."

"You're irresistible exactly the way you are."

She loved that he'd made all these preparations. If he hadn't been such a manly man, Molly would have told him that he was cute.

When she stepped into the outer room of the suite, she was amazed. A meal was laid out on the table. Around the suite, candles flickered. Roses were everywhere.

Inexplicably, she felt tears stinging the back of her eyelids. *He thought she was special.*

Adam gestured broadly. "Operation Cupid's Arrow."

"I'm touched." She wiped the tears away. All he had to do to get her into his bed was to tell her that she was needed. "This is fantastic."

"If you'd taken a bath when I'd told you to," he said, "it would have been more impressive."

"Everything is perfect."

They dined on one of her favorite meals. Lobster with drawn butter, asparagus and green salad with raspberry vinaigrette dressing. The flavors were absolutely sensual. Even more sexy was the fact that Adam had noticed, after all these years, what she liked to eat. By candlelight, they sipped fine, fizzy champagne.

As she licked the last bite of chocolate mousse from her lips, Molly whispered, "I think the bed might be getting cold."

"I know how we can warm it up."

"Take me."

And he did. Twice more.

Afterward, they lay quietly side by side, allowing the enormity of what had passed between them to settle.

Molly wasn't ready to question or second-guess their lovemaking. She didn't care what it meant in terms of greater implications. For right now, at this moment, she was as close to happiness as she'd ever been.

Chapter Seventeen

Adam finally got to wear his tuxedo when they left their hotel suite the following afternoon. As he escorted Molly to the grand staircase leading into the Brown Palace lobby, he knew he was looking good in spite of the bulge from his shoulder holster.

And Molly was fantastic.

Back in their suite, he'd enjoyed watching her as she got ready for the wedding reception. She piled her hair on top of her head and added another chunk of matching blond curls on top. Her bright blue dress had a thigh-high slit and a plunging neckline. She was wearing pearls. Lots of pearls. Three long necklaces and a huge bracelet of pearls with several strands circling her slender arm.

Slowly, they descended the staircase. Heads turned in their direction, and he was proud to be with the most beautiful woman in the room—the most beautiful woman in the world. He leaned close to her ear and whispered, "You look great."

She gazed up him. Her eyes were still that dreamy shade of blue that came with making love, but her voice held a teasing note. "Finally, you know the right thing to say when I'm all dressed up."

He'd always thought she was pretty. Until now, it hadn't seemed right to tell her. "I'm not making a compliment because I'm supposed to. You're truly lovely."

"And you're very classy in your tux," she said.

He nodded. It was a good thing that Operation Cupid's Arrow hadn't worked out exactly as he'd planned. If he'd worn his tux last night before they made love, Molly might have ripped off all the buttons.

His memory of that moment lingered in his mind like the taste of Courvoisier. Making love to Molly had temporarily quenched an unassuageable thirst, a thirst he had not even been aware of. And now, he was ready for more. He wanted to make love to her every day and every night. To live with her. To have children with her.

Whoa! Adam did a quick mental backpedal. Living together? Having babies? That sounded a lot like marriage. It might be prudent to take more time before he considered that step.

For most of his life, he'd been a bachelor. His brief marriage hardly even counted because he'd been out of the country on duty during three quarters of the time he'd been wed. His sensibilities were those of a bachelor, and he was even more set in his ways than most men. Adjusting to the constant presence of another person—even if that other person was Molly—wouldn't be easy.

He knew they'd maintain the teasing that had been part of their relationship for years. But would their differences turn into arguments? His greatest fear was that Molly would turn into his mother, and he would become his father.

No way. That transformation couldn't happen. Unlike his father, Adam controlled his temper just as he controlled his intake of alcohol—never more than a single glass, which he savored. And Molly was nobody's doormat.

And so…the next step. Marriage?

There was no rush. Molly wasn't going to disappear or anything. But he *wanted* to move forward. If he'd learned anything from the disruption of his plans last night, it was this: you can't plan for emotions. Every logistical detail could be thwarted by a whim, a feeling, a doubt, a fear.

Last night and this morning, he'd wanted to tell Molly he loved her. The words had climbed up his throat more than once. But he held his tongue. He didn't feel it was the perfect moment.

He escorted her toward the ballroom where tables were set with lavish centerpieces and a dance floor was cleared for action. Only a few of the guests had arrived from the church where the ceremony had taken place, but the waiters stood at the ready. The first person to approach Molly and Adam was Denny Devlin.

Ignoring Adam, he spoke to Molly in a panicky, quavering tone. "Where are they? The ice sculpture is melting."

"I'm not in charge," she said. "You'll have to talk to Gloria."

"If I could find her." When he scowled, his chef hat slipped lower on his forehead. "I have a very special arrangement with the staff here. I'm one of the only outside caterers they use, and they wouldn't allow me in the building after that…you know."

"The hepatitis incident," Adam said, cheerfully reminding him of the debacle that nearly ruined his career.

"Shhhhh." Denny glanced to the left and right, wary of encroaching viral infections. "Anyway, it's vital for everything to be perfect."

"I'm sure it'll be fine," Molly said. "By the way, I came across a name, and I wondered if you've ever heard of this person. Phil Prath."

At the mention of the mysterious person who rented the downtown loft, Adam watched Denny's reaction. Though the caterer was already wound tighter than the mainspring on a Swiss watch, he was visibly startled.

Denny shook his head in denial. "Never heard of him."

"I think you have," Molly pressed. "I think you know exactly who I'm talking about."

"I'm warning you," he said, "leave this alone."

Denny pivoted swiftly and raced back toward the table with the ice sculpture that had already morphed into something resembling a blobby snowman.

When Molly leaned toward him, Adam caught a whiff of her perfume. Today's fragrance was spicy and tantalizing. It reminded him of sex.

Quietly, she said, "Denny's in on the crime. He knows Phil Prath."

"I don't like the warning," Adam said. "I'd feel a lot better if you were carrying a gun."

"It wouldn't fit in my purse," she said.

He eyed the crescent-shaped purse of blue-and-white leather. "It's plenty big enough for a .22 caliber pistol."

"But I need my cell phone and my keys and lipstick. A gun would make an ugly bulge. Did you notice that the purse matches my shoes?"

Another pair of ridiculously high heels, unsuitable for sprinting. "I want you to stay close to me, Molly. Don't go wandering off by yourself."

He'd been so intoxicated by last night that he'd almost forgotten the real reason they were here. According to the anonymous note, the crime was set for this afternoon. Any minute now.

As guests poured into the ballroom, Adam switched to a supervigilant mode. He scanned faces in the crowd, needing to be aware of every move, every nuance.

He and Molly probably should have gone to the church to stake out the actual ceremony, but that was a more controlled setting, and he had confidence in the abilities of Tony and the other CCC volunteers who would help Lucien Smythe guard the necklace.

Still, when Heidi and her groom entered the ballroom to applause, Adam was relieved. The little bride was wearing the diamonds.

"Wow!" Molly said. "That necklace is amazing."

Though jewelry didn't generally impress him, Adam had to agree. Several strands of diamonds hung from a fancy latticework of gleaming white gold.

"And look," Molly said smugly. "She didn't change my suggestions for the gown."

Heidi glittered from the top of her veil to the hem of her skirt. If the sparkles stitched onto the fabric had been real, her bridal outfit would have been worth another eight hundred thousand dollars.

Adam was pleased to see Tony and two other CCC volunteers standing close to the bridal party. In their tuxedos and dress shoes, these retired military men fit in very nicely with the rest of the crowd. Maneuvering subtly, they managed to stay within an arm's length of Heidi at all times.

Lucien Smythe brought up the rear. He came directly toward them. After shaking Adam's hand and gallantly kissing the tips of Molly's fingers, he said, "I've never had such effective security. Thank you for making the arrangements."

Molly accepted the compliment. "Your necklace looks perfect with Heidi's gown."

"I never would have suggested more glitter," he said. "But you're right. She told me that she was supposed to look like a snow princess, and I believe she does."

"What's the procedure with the necklace?" Adam asked. "What happens if Heidi leaves this room to powder her nose?"

"She'll be accompanied up to her room," Lucien said. "No public restrooms, of course."

"And when the reception is over?"

"Very simple. We escort Heidi to her room, and she hands over the jewels. Your men will return to the store with me."

The plan seemed simple and straightforward. If stealing the necklace was the intended crime, Adam couldn't imagine how the thieves would pull it off.

Before Lucien departed, he glanced between Molly and Adam. "It's a shame that Molly is engaged to someone else. You make a handsome couple."

"Thank you," Molly said.

She glanced down at the engagement ring that had once belonged to Adam's mother. All too soon, she'd have to return these lovely diamonds to their resting place in the CCC wall safe. She couldn't be an undercover bride forever.

Though it had been fun to pretend that she was getting married, the exercise was superficial and wearing on her nerves—even more after last night with Adam. When he held her after they'd made earthshaking love, she felt different than ever before. Safe in his arms, she wondered if she'd finally found her mate, the man she was supposed to be with for the rest of her life.

All these years, true love had been right under her nose. Who knew?

As the ballroom began to fill up, waiters in white

jackets circulated with glasses of champagne and trays of hors d'oeuvres. Some of the guests were finding their places at the tables.

As she and Adam milled at the edge of the growing crowd, Molly caught a glimpse of Gloria, who seemed to be having a very intense conversation with Denny Devlin. Were they talking about Phil Prath? Would Gloria take Denny's warning to the next level?

Beside her, Adam groaned and said, "This is going to take forever."

"I'm afraid so." There were all the wedding reception rituals to go through. "The cutting of the cake. The toasts. The first dance by the bride and groom. Not to mention the dinner."

Under his breath, he said, "Maybe we should go back up to our room for a while."

Though the thought was tempting, she turned him down. "We haven't done all this investigating to back off now. Something's up. I can feel it."

"Molly, nobody is going to steal that necklace. Not with three armed guards and Lucien standing guard. If that was the planned crime, it's been foiled."

"What if it's something else?"

She directed him toward Stan Lansky who stood quietly beside an attractive young woman who Molly recognized from her photo. "Hi, Stan. This must be your wife."

"Tammy," he introduced her proudly.

With a bright smile, she shook Molly's hand. "I love weddings, don't you?"

"I do," Molly said. "Your dress is gorgeous. Did Stan make it for you?"

Tammy gave a twirl and her lacy pink gown fluttered delicately around her. "My husband is a genius. He should be a designer."

"He does good work," Molly agreed. "The extra sparkles on Heidi's gown are terrific. She looks like a million bucks."

"I have an idea," Tammy said.

She seemed so young that Molly halfway expected her to suggest a game of jump rope. "What's that?"

"You're getting married," Tammy said, pointing to the engagement ring. "You could use Stan as your designer."

With both of them gazing up at her expectantly, she couldn't refuse. "I promise, Stan. When I get married, you'll be the one who designs my gown."

"And you can have all the sequins you want," he said.

When he was with Tammy, his personality changed completely. He went from a rabbity, nervous man to a worldly sophisticate.

As she and Adam strolled away, she muttered, "This just gets worse and worse. We really haven't figured out anything. The jewels are safe—"

"You sound disappointed about that."

"Of course I'm not." If they'd prevented a crime, that should be satisfaction enough. "But we still don't know who attacked Pierce. Or me. And we still don't know why."

"It's a little vague," Adam said.

"And now, Stan and Tammy are all excited about my impending wedding to the nonexistent kangaroo farmer. I'm such a fraud."

She stood quietly for a moment. The several bridesmaids, including the pregnant one, scattered through the room like petals from a pink taffeta rose. Everyone seemed so happy.

Molly herself had ample reason to be cheerful. Her

new relationship with Adam should have been enough to make her smile. But she felt deflated.

Adam cleared his throat. "Have I mentioned how great you look?"

"Thanks for trying to make me feel better, but all the compliments in the world aren't going to clean up this investigation." All the pieces were there. She just couldn't put them together into a coherent solution. "I guess I'm not much good as a detective."

Adam didn't answer. He didn't build up her ego with false praises. That wasn't his way. Adam was always and forever truthful.

He offered, "Can I get you a drink?"

"I'd love a glass of champagne."

"Be back in a sec," he said. "Don't go anywhere."

Of course, she'd be standing right here, unmoving and uninspired. She watched the ebb and flow of the guests as they crossed the room, meeting and greeting each other. The arrangement of tables at the edge of the dance floor created a bottleneck, and that was where Stan was standing.

Molly focused on him as he turned away from Tammy for a moment and bumped against another couple. If Molly hadn't been a pickpocket herself, she might not have noticed that Stan had lifted the other man's wallet.

"Well, well," she murmured. Stan Lansky was the magpie, after all. Returning her pen had been a ruse.

She edged toward him, intending to confront him with the evidence. But Stan had moved away. He'd left Tammy on the floor, chatting happily with one of the bridesmaids while he edged toward the exit.

Molly glanced quickly over her shoulder. She ought to find Adam and tell him where she was going, but she couldn't let Stan get away with the evidence. As long as he had that wallet in his pocket, she had proof that he was the magpie.

Pushing her way toward the exit, Molly felt a firm grip on her arm. She spun around. "Ronald."

"Going somewhere?" His eyes were cold. "You know, sweetie, I still can't believe you were investigating me. *Moi?* I'm so totally innocent."

"You haven't been innocent since the day you were born," she said. "Let go of my arm."

"Honey, we need to chat."

"Not unless you're willing to tell me the truth." She kept her eye on the exit. Stan was almost there. He'd been stopped for a moment by Gloria.

"Before I tell you, I want to be sure you're not going to the real police."

She wrenched away from him. There wasn't time to be pleasant and glib. "Does this have anything to do with Phil Prath?"

Ronald shuddered. His lips pinched tightly together. "It's not my fault. Gloria made me do it."

"Do what?"

"A fake identification. No big deal."

"For Phil Prath?"

"And a few others. They were Gloria's friends from Thailand, and she insisted. Sweetie, it was almost like a joke."

"Not funny," she said. There were many other questions she needed to ask, but not right now.

"Molly, sweetheart, please try to understand."

"We'll talk later."

She raced toward the exit. Stan was getting away, and she had only one chance to catch him with the stolen wallet.

Chapter Eighteen

Molly tailed Stan Lansky as he crossed the lobby and left the Brown Palace. At dusk on a Saturday in downtown Denver, she was finally doing the work of a real detective—pursuing a thief with the evidence of his crime tucked in the trouser pocket of his immaculately tailored suit.

She stayed half a block behind Stan, dodging behind lampposts and mingling with other pedestrians. Though her fancy blue dress and ropes of pearls made her an obvious standout in a crowd, Stan hadn't seemed to notice her. The few times he glanced over his shoulder, she'd been careful to duck behind someone taller.

Her skills at tailing and surveillance were lousy, and she couldn't believe he hadn't spotted her. What if he had seen her? What if he meant for her to follow? This could all be a ruse. He might be luring her into an ambush.

She scanned the well-lit streets between tall buildings, looking for danger and finding nothing more ominous than a number fifteen bus. Molly took the cell phone from her purse and speed-dialed the phone she knew was in Adam's tuxedo pocket.

"Where the hell are you?" he demanded.

"I saw Stan take a wallet. I'm tailing him."

"Damn it, Molly. I gave you one instruction: stay put. Was that so hard to—"

"I'm heading north on Seventeenth," she said. "And I'm not turning back. Stan has the wallet. That's proof. He's the magpie."

Stan didn't frighten her. Perhaps he should. He had to be crazy to think he could get away with another magpie theft when security in the ballroom was so tight. Stan knew about the extra guards; he'd been in Gloria's shop when she made the arrangements for Tony and the other CCC guards to accompany Lucien Smythe.

Was Stan crazy? Or smart like a fox. With all the attention focused on the diamond necklace, it might be a very clever time to pick a pocket or two.

That little creep! She stepped up her pace on the sidewalk as he approached the corner. Moments before he stole the wallet, he'd been chatting with Molly and smiling. He'd promised to sew her a wedding gown with plenty of sparkle. And all the while, he was plotting his next theft.

He slipped into a multistory parking structure, and she reported to Adam, "He's going into the EZ Park Garage."

"Don't follow him. I'll be there in two minutes."

But she couldn't stay back. She had to see where Stan was going, and she damn sure wouldn't let him get away with his loot.

Inside the garage, her high heels clicked loudly on the concrete, and she paused to take them off and carry them. Her annoyance at Stan racheted up a few notches. Her panty hose were going to be ruined.

Hiding behind parked cars, she followed Stan as he hiked up the ramp to the second level. Halfway up, he stopped behind a late model gray sedan and plugged his key into the lock for the trunk.

Molly ducked behind an SUV and watched.

Calmly, Stan removed the stolen wallet from his pocket. As he sorted through the contents, she glimpsed a furtive smile on his face. He took out the cash and discarded the wallet on the floor of the parking garage.

Then, he opened his trunk and reached inside to rearrange the contents. A brand new toaster. A Mixmaster still in the box. A shiny silver tray.

He stood up straight and dug into his pockets—which must have been specially tailored to be exceptionally deep. Stan pulled out a couple of silver place settings. More loot.

He was, without doubt, the thief.

From outside the garage, Molly heard the endless rumble of traffic on the downtown streets. In here, Stan was humming. Though she didn't recognize the tune, the melody sounded upbeat. He was happy, almost giddy.

In his black suit and white shirt, his coloring reminded her of a magpie, cackling over small, stolen treasures. Bits of string and foil. Shiny objects.

Stan Lansky was a very strange bird.

When he slammed the trunk and went around to the driver's side door, Molly knew she had to stop him. She couldn't allow him to drive away with the evidence.

She stood. In a loud, firm voice, she said, "It's over, Stan."

He whirled around. His shoulders hunched and he squinted though the garage was well-lit. "Molly?"

"You're the one who's been stealing things from the weddings." She strode toward him, gesturing angrily with her shoe. "I saw you pick that man's pocket at the Brown Palace."

"Your word against mine," he said.

"Stan, the inside of your trunk is stuffed with loot."

He darted toward his trunk as though he intended to shield his treasures from her with his body. "What does it matter? The rich people won't miss these things. I deserve them."

"You stole—"

"I work hard," he said. "I cater to their whims, listen to their whining and complaining. They have everything. It's not fair."

Life wasn't fair. Molly would agree with that. "But you can't steal to even out the balance."

"I've never taken anything precious to them. I've heard them talking after a theft. They laugh. They say it isn't important."

"You hear everything, don't you?" She remembered him quietly going about his business while Gloria flounced dramatically around her boutique. "You know all the secrets."

"Yes," he hissed.

"You're the one who put that note in my purse," she said.

"Maybe I did."

Stan Lansky had all the answers. He was the key to opening up her investigation. She had a million questions, but she focused on the most important. "What's going to happen? What is the crime?"

"It's bad, very bad. I wanted to get away before anything happened. To take Tammy home."

"Tell me, Stan." There might still be time to prevent disaster.

"It's not wrong for me to steal," he said petulantly.

Molly wasn't interested in a discussion of ethics. "Work with me. Tell me your secret."

"I steal for Tammy. When I bring her gifts, she's so happy." His features crumpled with an attempted smile. "She's like a kid at Christmastime."

Molly heard a clicking sound from the high end of the parking ramp. Was it Adam? On bare feet, she moved closer to Stan. "Tammy would want you to tell me about this crime. She'd want to stop it."

He straightened his narrow shoulders. "Are you going to turn me in?"

She thought back to seven years ago, when she'd stolen from Adam and he'd given her another chance. It was within her power to let Stan go free with a promise that he'd never be the magpie again. "You'll have to make restitution."

"Not the police." He shuddered. "You can't turn me over to the police."

She stood only a few paces away from him. Her weight balanced lightly on the balls of her feet. If Stan made a move on her, she might be in serious trouble. Her long skirt, even with the slit, would get in the way of karate kicks. She hoped Adam would hurry.

"Molly," he said, "we can make a deal."

"What kind of deal?"

"You don't really care about these trinkets."

She nodded. He was right. Though she'd been initially drawn into this wedding miasma by the investigation of the magpie, there were more important issues. "Tell me what you know."

"And you'll let me go?"

"I'll do what I can."

"I know everything." He grinned. "I'm always there. Listening and watching. Nobody pays any attention to me. I'm just the tailor. The lackey. They talk. Oh my, they talk and talk. They make their plans, and I hear every word."

"Tell me."

"Not so fast." He held up his hand, signaling her to stay back. "You have to swear to let me go."

She struggled with her conscience, thinking of Adam, who would surely insist on turning Stan over to the cops. Detective Berringer would never honor any agreement she made with Stan. "I can't make that promise," she said. "It's out of my hands."

"I'll tell you about the real crime." Stan's voice took on a pleading note. "Gloria's crime."

Molly wanted to grab his shoulders and shake the truth out of him.

Stan glanced at his wristwatch. "There's not much time left."

Molly heard another clicking noise from higher up the ramp. A barrage of gunfire rang out. The sound echoed inside the concrete garage like thunder.

Stan wailed. His small, skillful hands clawed at his white shirtfront. It was red with blood. He slumped against the trunk of his car, protecting his treasures with what might be his last breath.

Molly leapt toward him as more gunfire erupted. She dragged Stan to the pavement between his car and the one parked beside it, hoping to protect him.

Too late, she realized that she'd trapped herself in the narrow space between the cars. If the shooter came after her, there was no escape.

She looked down at Stan, who was still breathing. "Tammy," he choked out the name. "I love her. I did it all for her."

"Don't talk," Molly whispered. "Save your strength."

She had to escape this trap. Unarmed, she was completely helpless against the gunman.

When she bobbed up behind the trunk to take another

look, there were more shots. Bullets pinged against the parked vehicles. Stepping over Stan, she went to the hood. The nose of the car beside him was parked too close to the concrete wall; she couldn't wedge her way through without presenting a target. But she had to move.

Acting on instinct, she dove across the hood and slid to the opposite side of the car, tumbling in a heap. Not a graceful move. But she'd made progress.

Unfortunately, the next car in line was a van. Not a white van. But a flat-nosed van that hemmed her in like a wall. If she got out of here alive, she intended to write a nasty letter to the manufacturer.

Her only chance for escape was to crawl under the van. Kissing her gorgeous blue dress goodbye, Molly went down flat on her back and wriggled on the hard concrete, inching her way under the van like a mechanic doing an oil change. Only two more cars, and she'd be at the end of the row. She could make a run for it.

Her long pearl necklace tangled in the undercarriage. She was stuck. *Damn it!* Struggling, she yanked at the necklace. These cheap pearls should break in a second, but the necklace felt strong as steel.

She heard a burst of gunfire. Then a single shot. And another.

Adam called out, "Molly, are you all right?"

"Go back."

Stuck under the van, she heard the sounds of pursuit. More gunfire. Then silence.

Adam! If he'd been shot, she might as well step into the light and tell the sniper to shoot her, too. She didn't want to live without Adam. He was the love of her life, the man she should be marrying.

"Molly," he said. "Where are you?"

The sound of his voice motivated her. With a yank, she snapped the pearls and fought her way out from under the van.

Higher up the concrete ramp, she saw Adam. He was kneeling beside the prone body of another man, but Adam appeared unharmed. Pure relief washed over her. Thank God, he was all right. If anything had happened to him, she would have died.

In her mind, she was running toward him. But her feet were slow to move. It felt as if she were in shock as she approached him.

When he stood and took out his cell phone, he turned toward her. There were splatters of blood on his white shirtfront.

"Are you hurt?" She came more swiftly toward him. "Adam, are you all right?"

"I'm fine," he said tersely. He spoke into the phone, giving instructions to the 911 dispatcher. Then he knelt again beside the man he'd been forced to shoot. "He's still alive."

"Who is he?" Molly asked.

"I don't know. He's unconscious."

Adam stood. He holstered his sidearm and tightened his fists to control the tremors that radiated up and down his arm. What the hell was going on with him? It couldn't be fear. He'd never been afraid for himself. Molly's safety was another matter entirely.

When he'd approached the garage and heard gunfire, he'd felt panic—the ice-cold chill of a terror he had never experienced before. Not in combat. Not in any circumstance.

If she'd been shot... He shook himself, not wanting to face that dire possibility. He reined in his emotions, set aside his fear and turned toward her.

She was a mess. Her shoes were gone. Her hair tumbled down around her face. And her dress was filthy.

He smiled. "You're beautiful."

She leapt into his arms, clinging tightly as though she'd never let go. And that was fine with him. He couldn't imagine a better future than to be with Molly night and day. "I love you," he said.

"Oh, Adam." She released her stranglehold. Her blue eyes shone brightly. "I love you back."

Once again, he might have chosen a better place and time to make this declaration. He should have been standing by a waterfall with birds chirping in the background.

Instead, they were in a concrete garage. One man lay injured at their feet. And Stan Lansky was making loud groaning noises.

Molly glanced down at the sniper. "You're not going to get in trouble for shooting him, are you?"

"Self-defense," he said. He pointed toward a high corner of the garage near the ceiling. "I'm sure it's all been caught on videotape."

"Too bad this guy is unconscious," she said. "He could have answered some questions."

"We've got one answer already," Adam said.

"What's that?"

"We suspected that a professional assassin stabbed Pierce in his office. This sniper fits the bill."

She broke away from Adam's embrace and knelt down beside the unconscious man. Without the slightest hesitation, she plunged her hand into his trouser pocket.

"What are you doing?" Adam asked.

"Looking for identification," she said. "There's got to be some kind of clue."

"Wait for the cops, Molly. From now on, it's their investigation."

"I don't think so." She dug into another pocket. "Right before Stan was shot, he promised to tell me about the crime. He said it was Gloria's crime, and there wasn't much time left. Something is going to happen now. Immediately."

She found a wallet and handed it to Adam. While Molly continued to search, he flipped it open. "Colorado driver's license."

"Is he Phil Prath?"

"His name is John Simpson."

Adam ran his thumb across the laminated surface of the card. There was something wrong with this identification. The mountains in the background were a strange shade of blue, almost turquoise. And the name, John Simpson, didn't fit the sniper who looked Asian. "This might be a fake."

Molly looked up, wide-eyed. "Ronald said he'd made fake IDs. He said they were for Gloria's friends."

"When did you talk to Ronald?"

"In the ballroom. Just as I was leaving. He looked really nervous when I mentioned Phil Prath."

"I don't like the way this is shaping up," he said. "You mentioned Phil Prath to Ronald. And to Denny Devlin. Within minutes, you'd been attacked by a sniper."

She shook her head. "But he shot Stan Lansky. I was standing right there and he didn't—"

"What was happening when he shot Stan?"

She swallowed hard. "He was about to tell me about the crime."

Stan Lansky was the first victim, Adam thought. And Molly surely would have been the second. "Thank God you called me."

In the pocket of the sniper's blazer, she found a small flat booklet. "A passport." She opened it. "He's from Bangkok."

Adam had a sense that this was significant, but he couldn't remember why. "What's the connection?"

"The wedding gowns." Molly scrambled to her feet. "They're handsewn in Thailand."

"And?"

A brilliant smile lit Molly's face. "Gloria's crime is smuggling."

Chapter Nineteen

Molly heard the wail of sirens approaching the parking garage. There wasn't much time; she had to talk fast. But so many thoughts churned inside her brain that she couldn't find the words to explain her conclusion.

"Sparkles," she said. "Glitter."

Adam looked at her as though she'd taken leave of her senses. "Are we playing some kind of word association game? Charades?"

Frustrated by her own lack of coherence, she glared at him. In contrast to her own grease-stained appearance, he was incredibly cool. Adam stood there in his tuxedo with a semiautomatic gun in one hand, looking like a sexy movie star version of an action-adventure hero. An all-American James Bond.

"Remember," she said. "When you talked to Pierce in the hospital, he mentioned glitter."

"And we assumed he meant Lucien Smythe's diamond necklace."

"But it wasn't the necklace," she said. "Pierce was talking about the glitter on Heidi's wedding gown."

Why hadn't she made this connection before? When she'd been in Pierce's hospital room, Heidi had been chattering about how she wanted dozens of sparkles sewn onto her bridal gown. Molly should have figured it out. She should have known.

The cops would be here any second. She had to pull herself together. She clasped Adam's free hand and held on tight, grounding herself. Then, she said, "Gloria orders her gowns from Thailand where they're handsewn, supposedly with cheap decorative sparkles. But here's the trick: the gems are real. High-quality diamonds."

"Illegal diamonds. She's involved in a diamond smuggling operation," Adam said. Finally, he was on the same page with her. "This is big, Molly. Trading in illegal gems is a multimillion dollar business, especially now when international terrorists need to transfer their funds undetected from one country to another."

Molly shuddered. She hadn't even considered the terrorist aspect. "These stones are hidden in plain sight on the wedding gowns when they go through customs."

"Go on," Adam said. "What happens next?"

"When a dress arrives in Gloria's shop, she removes the gems, and Stan replaces them." She was absolutely certain that she was right about this. "The very first time I visited Gloria's shop, I noticed a dress that had just been delivered. It had loose threads in need of repair."

"Was Pierce in the room?"

"Yes. He must have noticed the threads." And Pierce must have known enough about his ex-wife's smuggling scheme to confront her. "He figured out what she was doing. That's why he was attacked."

Molly remembered how she and Adam worked out the probable logistics of what had happened in the assault on Pierce. He'd been facing the door, talking to someone. That someone was Gloria. Then, he was knocked unconscious from behind, then stabbed. Probably by the professional assassin who lay at their feet.

Molly's gaze lowered. Though she'd gone through this man's pockets, she hadn't looked at his face. His eyelids were closed. His complexion, sallow. She should have felt more sorry that he'd been shot and might be near death. Instead, she was detached. She had the attitude of a real detective. "Do you think it was him? Did he attack Pierce?"

"Yes," Adam said.

She tightened her grip on his hand, appreciating his decisiveness when she felt as if her brain were flitting like a hummingbird from one conclusion to the next. "But why did he use a knife?"

Adam held up the semiautomatic, a lethal-looking weapon. "This makes a lot of noise."

But a knife? The use of a high-carbon, stainless steel knife pointed toward Denny Devlin. How was he involved? Before Molly had a chance for any more thinking, the ambulance raced up the ramp in the parking structure.

For the next several minutes, the paramedics efficiently did their work, providing aid for Stan and the sniper, then loading them into the rear of the ambulance.

One of them approached Molly, "Are you okay, miss?"

"I'm fine. I just look like hell."

He didn't bother to say otherwise. With a wink, he tipped his cap and ran back toward the ambulance.

Frowning, Molly poked at the rat's nest on top of her head. She didn't dare look at the damage to her dress and her torn pearl necklaces. This outfit was never meant for crawling under parked cars.

She scanned the floor of the garage. "Somewhere around here, I dropped my purse and matching shoes."

"I knew those shoes were worthless for running," Adam muttered.

"Speed wasn't the problem. The heels made too much noise on the concrete."

She spotted the purse and the shoes. She was slipping into her pumps when two cop cars squealed into the garage.

In addition to her natural reticence about police interviews, Molly had another concern. She returned to Adam's side. "We can't spend a lot of time with the cops. We need to act quickly. Stan said something was going to happen soon."

"What's supposed to happen?"

"I'm not sure. What's the next logical step?"

Adam filled in the blank. "Let's assume that Gloria, the owner of a bridal boutique, isn't really an experienced diamond smuggler."

"Probably not," Molly said. Though she didn't like Gloria, she couldn't imagine her as an international criminal mastermind.

"That means she's working with someone else."

"And?"

"The next thing that should happen is Gloria turns over the smuggled gems to the real criminals and gets her payoff."

When Molly last saw Gloria, she was inside the Brown Palace ballroom, talking with Denny Devlin. Surely, she wouldn't make the exchange there. Not with a whole ballroom full of witnesses.

As Ted Berringer sauntered toward them, Molly deliberately turned away. She whipped her cell phone from her purse and punched in the number for the hospital. The phone in Pierce's room rang half a dozen times before it was picked up by a nurse.

"Is Pierce there?" Molly asked.

"I'm sorry," the nurse said. "He signed himself out."

"You're joking! He didn't look well enough to stand on his own two feet, much less to be out of the hospital."

"I agree, but he insisted. I took him downstairs in a wheelchair, put him in a cab and handed the cabby a note with the address where Pierce wanted to be dropped off."

"Do you remember that address?" Molly asked.

"I don't remember exactly, but it was downtown."

The loft! Pierce was going to the loft!

That had to be where Gloria would turn the gems over to the smugglers. But why was Pierce going there? Either he was involved with the smugglers or he was walking into an ambush. Molly suspected the latter. If Pierce went to that loft, he'd be in mortal danger.

She came toward Berringer who stood with his arms folded across his chest, watching as the crime scene forensic investigators fanned out across the garage. Police procedure could often be a tedious process, and they didn't have much time.

After exchanging a hostile hello with Berringer, she said, "Your forensic people are wasting their time. The whole incident was recorded by the surveillance cameras in the garage."

"Molly, Molly," he said, "you just won't quit telling me how to do my job."

"If you'd listened to me before, this shootout might have been avoided."

"Yeah?" His voice was harsh. "I don't see any stolen diamond necklaces."

"Maybe I didn't have the details right, but I knew something was going to happen."

"And how did you know?" he asked. "Somebody steal a pencil? Another anonymous note?"

She could stand here arguing with him or she could take action. Molly turned to Adam and said, "May I speak to you for a moment?"

He came with her as she walked away from Berringer. "What's up?"

"Pierce checked himself out of the hospital. He's on his way to the loft."

"Of course," Adam said. "The loft. That's where it's all going to come together."

"We've got to go there. Right now. This minute."

"Hold on." His voice was annoyingly calm. "We've done all we can. It's time to turn this investigation over to the police."

"Berringer? He's never moved fast in his life. We need action, not somebody who's going to stand around and whine."

"He can't ignore this," Adam said darkly. "Not with the terrorist implications. I'll give him the information, and he'll set the wheels in motion."

"There isn't time." She knew how the system worked. "Berringer will need to get a warrant. To call for backup. Maybe even to contact Homeland Security. We can't wait around."

"Give it up, Molly."

"I won't." Her head was spinning. She wasn't opposed to having someone else do the final assault, but they needed someone who could act now. Right this minute! "What about the Feds? We know people. We're CCC. I should be running this show."

He grasped both of her arms, compelling her to look into his eyes. His gaze was hard—very different from the warmth that radiated from him when they made love. She knew this look, Adam's military look. He was about to give her an order.

"Your investigation is over," he said firmly. "To continue would be foolish."

How could he say that? "Are you calling me a fool?"

"Of course not. I'm telling you that you're in over your head. There's a time to retreat and—"

"I know," she said. "When you can't win, retreat. But we've won, Adam. We figured it out. We have to go to the loft."

"Calm down. Everything's going to be fine."

"Don't," she said. "Don't you dare patronize me."

She couldn't believe that he was reverting back to his overbearing, demanding self. Not after all they'd been through. Not after last night. She'd slept in his arms. Only moments ago, he told her that he loved her.

"I won't let you go to that loft," he said. "It's irresponsible and dangerous."

"Now I'm irresponsible?"

He slid his hands up her arms to her shoulders, holding her down. "Listen to me, Molly. I don't want you to get hurt. When I heard gunfire from inside this garage, I almost had a heart attack. I can't lose you."

"But I'm investigating, Adam. I figured out this whole smuggling scheme, and I won't let my efforts be for nothing." Pierce could be killed. "Danger is part of the job."

He had the nerve to grin. "You sound like one of those TV detective shows."

"I'm serious." Anger hardened her resolve. "You've got to take me seriously."

"As a detective?"

As a detective and a human being. She was more than his cute blond assistant. "Why can't you understand this?"

"Come on, Molly. We both know you're not cut out for field investigation. You're too good a person. You want to believe everybody."

His negative opinion of her skills hurt, but she wasn't going to argue with him now.

Adam spoke in a calm voice as though she were a dim-witted child. "I'll inform Berringer about the loft and the priority need for his men to go there."

"Fine." But she had a different plan. And it didn't include waiting around for the inexorably slow grinding of the wheels of justice. Molly glided her arms inside Adam's jacket and gave him a hug. When she pulled away, she'd slipped his gun from his shoulder holster. Her skills at picking pockets came in handy from time to time.

MOLLY LEFT the garage while Adam and Berringer discussed the plan for storming the loft. Her escape had been simple and subtle. She'd faked a headache and gone to sit down. From there, it was only a few steps to the exit.

On the sidewalk, she ran in her high-heeled pumps, dodging the pedestrians. Pierce's loft was only a few blocks away in LoDo which was, on a Saturday night, a hotbed of singles activity. Fans who had attended a Rockies' game surged toward the many brew pubs. Though today was nothing special, there was a festival atmosphere.

Molly's inner turmoil was the very opposite of light-hearted. She was angry at Adam, furious. When he told her that he loved her, he apparently didn't mean that he loved her as an equal. He thought of her as some sort of wounded bird, someone who was incapable of taking care of herself and needed him to hold her together.

Well, fine! Let him stay in the parking garage with his cop buddies. Let them dither and wither until after everything had gone down.

She'd rescue Pierce in her own way.

On the street corner outside the loft building, she spotted Gloria. Molly's fears were confirmed. The exchange of the illegal diamonds was about to take place.

Before Molly could hide herself in the crowd, Gloria turned. Their eyes met. There was no turning back.

Striding briskly, Molly closed the distance between them. "You can't do this, Gloria."

"I have no idea what you're talking about."

"Diamonds." Molly's hand was in her purse. Her fingers closed around the grip of Adam's gun. "You've been using your handsewn gowns from Thailand to smuggle diamonds."

Gloria's dark eyes flicked nervously. She didn't appear to be armed. All she carried was a small purse. "I have to make this exchange. If I don't, they'll kill me."

"Or Pierce," Molly said.

Gloria's cool sophistication crumbled. Her lower lip trembled. "I never meant for Pierce to be hurt. He chose the wrong time to confront me, and that man—"

"Attacked him from behind," Molly said. "Stabbed him in the back."

"Pierce was only trying to help me." She drew a shaky breath. "Trying to protect me."

"He still loves you," Molly said. There was no other explanation for his behavior. "All that time in the hospital, he could have told the police what was going on. He could have turned you in. But no. He kept your secret."

"Because he knew, Molly. He knew these terrible men would hurt me if I didn't do exactly what they said."

Poor, brave, misguided Pierce. He'd been trying his best to save the woman he loved. "How did you get involved in all this?"

"It started with the loft. My Thai contacts said they needed a place where they could stay when they came to Denver. I set the lease for them through the phony Sylvan Company. One thing led to another until I was in too deep."

Though Molly was inclined to forgive mistakes in judgment, Gloria's criminal scheme was too big and too dangerous to brush aside. "I can't let you go through with this."

A couple on the sidewalk accidentally jostled her, and Molly's hand rose from her purse, showing the gun.

"My God," Gloria said. "Do you intend to shoot me?"

"If I need to." Molly nodded toward the entrance for the loft building. "Let's get off the street."

Inside the empty lobby, Gloria checked her wristwatch. "I need to go upstairs. I'm expected."

"Forget it. We'll stay here and wait for the cops."

Gloria had recovered enough of her poise to be pushy. She tossed her head, and her straight black hair shimmered. "Listen, Molly. The best thing is to let me complete this transaction. I have it all planned."

"Right down to your alibi," Molly said. "There are hundreds of people at Heidi's wedding reception who will swear that you were there all the time."

Her lips pinched together. "Yes."

"But I know the truth."

"God, you're a pest," Gloria snapped. "I mean, look at you. Your hair's a disaster. Your dress is filthy, which is no great loss because it's a cheesy little outfit anyway."

"But I have the gun," Molly pointed out. "Wouldn't you say this is the perfect accessory?"

"I wish I'd killed you when I jumped out of that van."

"That was you?"

"That's right, Little Miss Detective. I was the one who came after you in the parking lot. I wanted to scare you off before you figured out too much. And, by the way, that kick to my thigh really hurt."

"Good," Molly said with heartfelt satisfaction. "I thought it was Denny Devlin who attacked me.

"Denny's a coward. He was terrified that the knives could be traced back to him. Actually, they were a gift to me. I still had them at the boutique. Believe me, Molly, I had no idea that thug had found my knives or that he'd use them on Pierce."

"Stan saw all this, didn't he?"

"Stan Lansky?" Gloria shrugged. "I suppose so. I don't pay much attention to what Stan does unless his work is substandard."

Stan the Magpie had been disturbed enough by Gloria's scheme to report her. But he didn't want to lose his job, so he sent the anonymous note.

Though Molly didn't want to become too sympathetic toward Stan, his crimes were naughty. Gloria's plan was big, vicious and evil.

"What about Ronald Atchison?" Molly asked.

"I needed his skills. He doesn't know about the smuggling, but he made a few fake identifications for my Thai associates."

"Like Phil Prath."

Molly nodded. She was somewhat impressed with Gloria's organizational skills. She'd marshaled her resources and put together a workable plan, using many of the people she knew. If Pierce hadn't confronted her, she might have gotten away with it.

"For once, be smart," Gloria said. "Let me make the exchange. Then these smugglers can be taken into custody."

"And you get away with the payoff?"

"I suppose not. What a shame! I'll give up the cash and turn state's evidence. I'll testify against these thugs."

Her smile was smug. Her ego was so huge that she really couldn't believe that anything bad would happen to her.

"There's only one problem with your plan," Molly said.

"What?"

"Pierce checked himself out of the hospital. He's already here."

Chapter Twenty

For the third time, Adam tried to explain to Detective Berringer about Gloria and the diamond smuggling scheme. It wasn't going well. The whole idea of a bridal boutique owner involved with international smuggling lacked credibility.

The detective frowned. "But why does she send dresses to Thailand in the first place?"

"Something to do with the handiwork or the stitching or something." Adam was nearing the end of his patience. "How the hell would I know about wedding gowns?"

"You've made a lot of assumptions here," Berringer said. "Without much evidence."

"The sniper," Adam said. "The man who fired at Molly has a Thai passport."

"Which doesn't connect him to wedding planners."

"Damn it, man. Molly has been investigating inside the wedding business. What more connection do you need?"

"You understand my reluctance," Berringer said. "If I call in Homeland Security and this turns out to be a bunch of baloney, I'll look like a jerk."

"Fine," Adam said crisply. He'd wasted enough time dealing with Berringer. "I'm calling the FBI."

In past cases with CCC, Adam had often dealt with Special Agent Gary O'Hara—a man who trusted his word. O'Hara wouldn't hesitate to act on a tip from Adam, especially when it involved an international crime like diamond smuggling.

"Wait!" When Berringer held up his hand, he looked like a traffic cop trying to hold back a semitruck. "I'll take care of the situation. Give me the address for the loft."

"Then what?"

"You know the procedures. I'll call in for a warrant and alert the SWAT team."

A time-consuming process. Molly had been right when she said it would take too long for the police to swing into motion.

After Adam gave Berringer the address, he reached into the inner pocket of his tuxedo to get his cell phone. It wouldn't hurt to give O'Hara a call and get another expert opinion.

His hand brushed his shoulder holster. Something didn't feel right. He patted the leather. His gun was gone. Damn it, he should have noticed the weight difference, but his Glock automatic was only a couple of pounds fully loaded.

He knew immediately how he'd lost his weapon. Molly. She embraced him after he'd told her in no uncertain terms that their investigation was over. He'd thought her hug meant she agreed with him. Instead, she'd picked his pocket.

Adam strode down the ramp inside the parking lot

to the place he'd left Molly resting on a concrete bench. Of course, she wasn't there. She'd taken off on her own.

Though he should have been angry at her for not obeying his orders, Adam's frustrated rage was directed squarely toward himself. He'd been wrong. Molly's instincts about the police taking too long had been right. She'd made the smart move and left him in the dust, trying to reason with the unreasonable Berringer.

There was a lesson to be learned. He needed to listen to Molly, to respect her opinion, even when he didn't agree.

As he exited the parking structure and headed toward Pierce's loft at a run, Adam hoped he wouldn't be too late to tell her she'd been right.

IT WASN'T EASY for Molly to formulate a plan of action with Gloria. Neither woman trusted the other. In the cool, silent corridor outside Pierce's loft, they whispered back and forth.

"Give me the gun," Gloria said. "I'll make the exchange and threaten them with the gun until they let Pierce leave with me."

"No way am I giving you the gun," Molly said. "You tried to kill me."

"Don't be silly. I just wanted to scare you off."

Molly glared. "You came at me like a knife-wielding psycho."

"But I'm the one who got hurt. I have a huge bruise on my thigh from where you kicked me."

They had to stop bickering and take action. Molly wished that Adam were here. In spite of his overbearing tendencies, his plans were always confident. The chain of command was always clear.

Unfortunately, her place at the bottom of that chain seemed to be a permanent condition—one she couldn't live with.

Her worst fear had come true. Adam didn't respect her as an equal. Even after they'd made love all night, he had to be the boss. Uncompromising. Hard as granite. He had the nerve to patronize her and treat her like a dumb blonde. Her dreams for a relationship were over. She'd have to quit at CCC. If she got out of here alive…

She turned to Gloria. "Here's what we're going to do. I'll come with you as a bodyguard. I'll have my gun drawn and ready. Take care of your business as quickly as possible. We'll grab Pierce and get out of here."

"But you don't—"

"No discussion," Molly snapped. When she wanted to, she could be just as hardheaded as Adam. "This is the way it's going down. Open the damn door."

Gloria used her key on the lock. She pushed the door open. Molly followed close behind. The Glock automatic was in her hand. The safety was off. She remembered Adam telling her that there were fifteen rounds in this weapon. He'd fired at the parking garage. Two or three times? She probably had ten shots left.

There were two men in the room with Pierce, who sat in a leather chair, barely hanging on to consciousness. He looked miserable.

"I'm Molly Griffith." She raised her weapon. "I'm

here to make sure this exchange goes as scheduled and nobody gets hurt."

A sleek, handsome man in a dark pin-striped suit stepped away from the windows. His smile reminded her of a king cobra baring his fangs. "I'm Phil Prath, and I am happy to proceed with our business. Gloria? I believe you have something for me."

"Let me see the money first," she said.

Phil Prath nodded to his equally well-dressed associate who placed a small attaché case on the coffee table and opened it. Tidy stacks of banded hundred dollar bills filled the attaché. "Three hundred thousand."

Molly's eyes popped. She'd never seen anywhere near that much money in one place. It didn't even look real.

"And now," Phil Prath said smoothly, "it's your turn, Gloria."

She gestured nervously. "I need to go into the kitchen."

"Why?"

"You didn't think I'd carry the diamonds with me, did you? They're here in the loft."

Keeping an eye on Phil Prath and his associate, Molly followed Gloria toward the kitchen. She muttered, "Please don't tell me you did the totally cliché thing of hiding the diamonds in the ice."

"Give me a little credit," Gloria said. "I had to get the diamonds out of my possession as quickly as possible. This is where Denny Devlin came in handy."

She opened the freezer. From far in the back, she removed four white boxes with the Devlin Catering logo stamped on top. She carried them ceremoniously to the front room where she placed them on the coffee table near Pierce's knee.

When he glanced at Gloria, Molly saw a strange coldness in his gaze. Pierce hadn't yet said a single word.

Gloria explained as she pried open the boxes labeled as microwaveable gourmet dinners. "I didn't want to keep the diamonds at my home or my place of business. So I ordered these dinners from Denny Devlin. When he delivered to my boutique, I opened the boxes, slipped the diamonds inside and brought them here."

Pierce spoke up, "Did Denny know he was involved in smuggling?"

"Certainly not," she said. "I told no one."

She lifted out the frozen dinner sealed in plastic and pointed. "Voilà!"

There was nothing else inside the container.

"Perhaps," said Phil Prath, "this is the wrong box."

"I don't think so."

Gloria tore open the other containers and found nothing. She dashed back into the kitchen for the rest of the containers and started ripping them to pieces. Her eyes were frenzied. Gone was her sophistication and poise. This was a woman caught in the grip of mortal panic.

And Molly didn't feel much better. Though she was holding the gun, she wasn't sure she'd be a match for Prath and his associate. They looked like the kind of men who slaughtered half a dozen traitors before dinner.

Slowly, Pierce rose from the chair. His large body teetered precariously. "I have the diamonds, Prath. Now, you're dealing with me."

ADAM HAD GAINED ACCESS to the loft building by follow-ing another couple through the front door to the lobby. They had no hesitation in letting him in. Who would question a man in a tuxedo?

He took the elevator to Pierce's floor and hurried down the long hallway. He hoped that Molly had re-membered some of the lessons he'd taught her, starting with this one: if you enter a location that might be dan-gerous, leave the door open. You might need to make a quick escape.

He pushed lightly on the loft door. It was unlatched. Excellent!

Adam took his second gun from the ankle holster. Molly had teased him about being too well armed, too well prepared. But his habits had served him well in the past. The second gun was necessary.

If he'd been half as good at relationships as he was at strategy, he might have avoided this chase. He could have reasoned with Molly. He wouldn't have made her so angry that she'd try to take on these criminals by her-self.

He eased inside the door. His greatest advantage at this moment was the element of surprise, and he was careful to move silently toward the half partition sepa-rating the living room where they all were gathered.

Pierce was standing. Behind him were two stran-gers. Gloria knelt on the floor amid a clutter of white boxes. And Molly was closest to where Adam was standing. She was holding the Glock automatic braced in both hands.

Adam planned his moves. If it came to a shoot-out, he'd dive to the opposite side of the room from Molly to draw their fire in that direction. Unfortunately, from that angle, Pierce would be directly in his line of fire.

MOLLY FELT SICK to her stomach. How could Pierce betray her? She believed in him, trusted him. She never thought in a million years that he was only after the money.

"How did you find the diamonds?" she asked.

"For the past couple of weeks, I've suspected that my dear ex-wife was up to something," he said. "I thought it might have something to do with this loft. She really wanted it in the divorce settlement. Didn't you, Gloria?"

She didn't answer. Gloria knelt on the carpet. Tears streaked down her cheeks.

"Anyway," Pierce said, "I came up here to look around, and I got hungry. So I dug around in the freezer until I found one of the microwaveable dinners I liked. Lo and behold! Diamonds!"

"My God," Gloria whispered. "What have you done? You've killed us all."

"I tried to talk to you," Pierce said. "That night in my office, I wanted to come clean. But your henchman stabbed me in the back."

"One question," Molly interrupted. "Why the hell did you hire me?"

"The magpie thefts are unrelated to this," Pierce said. "I'm truly sorry you got involved, Molly."

"We're all sorry," said Phil Prath. "And where are the diamonds?"

"I'll take you there," Pierce said. "And I want another three hundred thousand in cash."

"No," Prath said. "You will tell me where the gems

are hidden. I will fetch them. And we will never see each other again."

"I'm not going to tell you," Pierce said.

"You're making this very unpleasant," Prath warned.

Molly agreed. "Don't be a moron, Pierce. Do what he says."

"But if I tell him, what's to stop him from killing us all right now?" Pierce braced his hand on the back of the chair. He was obviously weak. "My way is better."

"I give you one more chance to tell me," Prath said.

Brashly, Pierce confronted him. "Or what? What are you going to do? You can't kill me. If I'm dead, you'll never find the diamonds."

Prath exhaled an impatient breath. He strode two paces toward the center of the room. Very quickly, he unholstered a sidearm which he pointed directly into Gloria's face. "If you don't tell me, I'll kill her."

Molly raised her gun, holding it on Prath.

He didn't flinch, didn't bat an eyelash. "You're outnumbered, Molly Griffith."

From the corner of her eye, she saw his associate. He was armed, and his gun pointed at Molly. They were at a standoff.

Molly played her ace card. "The police know. I told them about the loft, and they'll be here any minute."

A frown creased Prath's features. "I don't believe you."

"You'd better run," she said. "If you hurry—"

"Not without the gems," he said. "Pierce, you have three seconds before this woman dies."

"Tell him," Molly pleaded. "Pierce, tell this man what he wants to know."

"One… Two…"

She saw a blur on the opposite side of the room. Someone else was here. A shot rang out.

In slow motion, Molly saw Prath raise his weapon to aim at the other person. Molly's index finger tightened on the trigger of the Glock automatic. Gunfire echoed and exploded. She was standing so close to Prath that the force of the bullet penetrating his shoulder knocked him back a pace. He fell to the floor.

With the Glock braced in front of her, she wheeled toward Prath's associate. But he was already wounded, writhing on the floor as Adam kicked the weapon away from his hand.

Adam! Thank God, he was here.

He issued orders. "All of you, step out of the way. Molly, call 911."

She did as he said, helping Gloria to her feet. They went toward the kitchen. Pierce staggered toward them. His step was shaky, but he made it to the kitchen table where he sank into a chair and leaned forward, burying his face in his arms.

Molly made the 911 call and watched as Adam disarmed Prath and the other man, patting them down to search for other weapons. He didn't take his eyes off these dangerous adversaries for one second. Over his shoulder, he said to Molly, "You were right about coming here. You made the right call."

She nodded.

"Forgive me?" he asked.

"I owe you," she said. "You saved my life."

"But you're not going to let me off the hook." He glanced quickly toward her. "Go ahead and say it."

"I told you so."

"And I'm the fool for not listening."

It took a big man to admit his mistakes, but Molly couldn't dismiss a pattern of behavior that had taken root for seven years. She couldn't be with Adam if he didn't accept her as an equal. "If we're not compatible, it's better to find out now."

She couldn't believe they were having their first relationship talk while Adam held a gun on two bad guys who had tried to kill them.

"We're compatible," Adam said. "I can make changes. Hell, I want to make changes for you, Molly."

"You'll pay attention to my opinions?"

"Yes," he said.

"And you'll let me do more field investigating?"

"It's a deal, partner."

Partner? She hadn't thought that far ahead. "When you say partner, do you mean—"

"Fifty-fifty," he said. "I should have done this a long time ago. You do more than half the work at CCC. You should be equal with me."

"Then I forgive you."

In the midst of gore and chaos, she saw only him. Adam, her mentor. Adam, her partner. Adam, her one true love.

"What's going on?" Gloria demanded. "Molly, I thought you were engaged to some Aussie with kangaroos."

"Wrong," Molly said. "Adam Briggs is the only man I've ever truly loved."

The police came through the door with guns drawn, and Adam stepped aside.

Molly met his gaze. She recognized the warmth in

his eyes as he came toward her, pulled her into his arms and gave her a kiss that lifted her off her feet.

He whispered, "I love you, Molly. I want you to be a permanent part of my life."

"Yes," she said.

"Be my bride."

"Oh, yes."

She kissed him with all her heart. Their love was no longer undercover.

❖ SILHOUETTE®
INTRIGUE™

THE SHERIFF'S DAUGHTER
by Jessica Andersen

Medical investigator Logan Hart could never resist a damsel in distress. And seeing bullets fired at Samantha Blackwell brought out all of his protective instincts. But soon some chilling new evidence came to light... Was the target really Samantha, or Logan?

HER ROYAL BODYGUARD by Joyce Sullivan

Crown Prince Laurent Falkenburg was determined to protect Rory Kenilworth, even if that meant disguising himself as her guard and denying the attraction between them. Because this beautiful Californian girl was much more than a new princess threatened by assassins...she was *his* betrothed.

LAWFUL ENGAGEMENT
by Linda O Johnston
Shotgun Sallys

Cara Hamilton's reporter's instinct could smell the corruption in Mustang Valley, but she needed sexy lawman Mitchell Steele on her side to get the job done. Mitch wanted to prove his father had been murdered, and teaming up with Cara was no hardship, but would truth, justice and love prevail on judgement day?

MYSTIQUE by Charlotte Douglas
Eclipse

Trish Devlin had gone undercover at the exclusive Endless Sky resort to find the truth about her sister's disappearance. But the plot only thickens when Trish meets the enigmatic and attractive O'Neill. With more questions at every turn, can she get to the bottom of *all* of Endless Sky's mysteries?

On sale from 18th August 2006
www.silhouette.co.uk

Coming soon from No. 1 *New York Times* bestselling author Nora Roberts...

Atop the rocky coast of Maine sits the Towers, a magnificent family mansion that is home to a legend of long-lost love, hidden emeralds— and four determined sisters.

Catherine, Amanda & Lilah

available 4th August 2006

Suzanna & Megan

available 6th October

Available at WHSmith, Tesco, ASDA, Borders, Eason, Sainsbury's and all good paperback bookshops

www.silhouette.co.uk

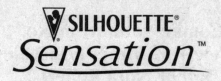

SILHOUETTE® *Sensation*™

PENNY SUE GOT LUCKY by Beverly Barton

The Protectors

When an eccentric millionaire leaves her riches to her beloved dog, Lucky, Penny Sue Paine is assigned as his guardian. But it seems someone wants this pooch dead. Enter Vic Noble, a gorgeous ex-CIA operative hired as Lucky's protector. Suddenly Penny Sue thinks *she's* the one who got lucky!

THE INTERPRETER by RaeAnne Thayne

Mason Keller took the unconscious woman he found in the middle of the road to recover at his ranch. Jane Withington couldn't remember why she was in Utah, but her language skills were superior…and her attraction to Mason was undeniable. As they tried to uncover her identity, could they escape the terrible threat from ruthless terrorists?

WILD FIRE by Debra Cowan

The Hot Zone

Firewoman Shelby Fox witnessed a murder and her life was plunged into danger. As she and old friend Detective Clay Jessup hunted a killer, an attraction between them which had long lain dormant burst into flames, and everything changed…

On sale from 18th August 2006

Available at WHSmith, Tesco, ASDA, Borders, Eason, Sainsbury's and most bookshops

www.silhouette.co.uk

SILHOUETTE®
Sensation™

0806/18b

SOMETHING WICKED by Evelyn Vaughn

Bombshell: The Grail Keepers

Kate Trillo cursed her sister's killer, but in doing so had cursed herself. And now it seemed that she might even have cursed the *wrong* man. Kate would have to delve into her heritage and find a long-lost goddess grail to learn the truth. But would the truth see that justice was done?

THE MAKEOVER MISSION
by Mary Buckham

When librarian Jane Richards ended up in an island kingdom with Major Lucas McConneghy, she was at a loss as to what he could want with *her*, until she saw it was her stunning similarity to the queen that had brought her there. And with danger lurking everywhere Lucas might be protecting her, but he was putting her heart at a greater risk...

FLAWLESS by Michele Hauf

Bombshell: The IT Girls

An elite jeweller had been shot, diamonds embedded with military secret codes were missing...and the Gotham Rose spy and gemologist Becca Whitmore was on the case. Blazing a trail through Europe with her partner, MI-6 agent Aston Drake, to find the stones and the shooter, could Becca stop the codes from falling into the wrong hands, before it was too late?

On sale from 18th August 2006

Available at WHSmith, Tesco, ASDA, Borders, Eason,
Sainsbury's and most bookshops

www.silhouette.co.uk

FREE

2 BOOKS AND A SURPRISE GIFT!

We would like to take this opportunity to thank you for reading this Silhouette® book by offering you the chance to take TWO more specially selected titles from the Intrigue™ series absolutely FREE! We're also making this offer to introduce you to the benefits of the Mills & Boon® Reader Service™—

- ★ **FREE home delivery**
- ★ **FREE gifts and competitions**
- ★ **FREE monthly Newsletter**
- ★ **Books available before they're in the shops**
- ★ **Exclusive Reader Service offers**

Accepting these FREE books and gift places you under no obligation to buy; you may cancel at any time, even after receiving your free shipment. Simply complete your details below and return the entire page to the address below. You don't even need a stamp!

YES! Please send me 2 free Intrigue books and a surprise gift. I understand that unless you hear from me, I will receive 4 superb new titles every month for just £3.10 each, postage and packing free. I am under no obligation to purchase any books and may cancel my subscription at any time. The free books and gift will be mine to keep in any case.

I6ZEE

Ms/Mrs/Miss/Mr...Initials ....
                                                                          BLOCK CAPITALS PLEASE

Surname ....

Address ....

....

....Postcode ....

Send this whole page to:
The Reader Service, FREEPOST CN81, Croydon, CR9 3WZ